GRINDER

GRINDER

MIKE **KNOWLES**

ECW Press

Published by ECW Press
2120 Queen Street East, Suite 200, Toronto, Ontario, Canada M4E 1E2
416.694.3348 / info@ecwpress.com

LIBRARY AND ARCHIVES CANADA CATALOGUING IN PUBLICATION

ISBN: 978-1-55022-895-3

Knowles, Mike
Grinder / Mike Knowles.

I. Title.

PS8621.N67G74 2009   C813'.6   C2009-902537-X

Editor: Edna Barker
Cover and Text Design: Tania Craan
Cover Image © George Cairns / iStockphoto
Typesetting: Mary Bowness
Printing: Friesens   1   2   3   4   5

The publication of *Grinder* has been generously supported by the Canada
Council for the Arts which last year invested $20.1 million in writing and
publishing throughout Canada, by the Ontario Arts Council, by the
Government of Ontario through Ontario Book Publishing Tax Credit,
by the OMDC Book Fund, an initiative of the Ontario Media
Development Corporation, and by the Government of Canada through
the Book Publishing Industry Development Program (BPIDP).

 Canada Council   Conseil des Arts
for the Arts   du Canada
 Canadä   ONTARIO ARTS COUNCIL
CONSEIL DES ARTS DE L'ONTARIO

PRINTED AND BOUND IN CANADA

ECW PRESS
ecwpress.com

For Andrea.
It could be for no one else.

CHAPTER ONE

I saw him before he even thought I might be the one he was looking for. In one moment all the months of work, honest work, that I thought had worn down what I was, proved worthless. I saw him, out of place on the wharf. His clothing was too metrosexual to be local, and too dance club to be tourist. The jeans were expensive and artificially worn in around the thighs and crotch. His shirt was not cotton, but rather some kind of stretchy blend that stood out unnaturally in the sunlight. The worst was the shoes, their leather shiny and the tips pointed. I knew he was an outsider, and part of me, the part I tried to bury, knew exactly where he was from.

I saw him, but he couldn't see me — not yet. The ocean had changed me enough. I was leaner, harder, and my skin was the colour of worn leather. My hair was long under my hat and my beard was far past the scratchy stage. My clothes were old and worn. I made sure I looked like everyone else who lived on the island before I left the house each day. As I walked around the boat getting ready to offload the day's haul, I watched the out-of-place man. He didn't see me yet, but he would. I was two thousand kilometres from home and too jaded to believe in coincidences. He wasn't here by accident. He knew I was here, and my fisherman's camouflage wouldn't make me invisible forever. I had to make him see me and make him move on me here. If he had known where I lived, he would have been waiting for me there. He was at the wharf looking to set up a tail. I was still one step ahead. That picture brought him here — that damn picture. I had to make sure here was where he stayed.

left Hamilton in stages. The first stage was getting out of the standoff in Paolo Donati's restaurant. Paolo, my former employer, had sent men to bring me to him. I had railroaded the soldiers he sent into letting me drive myself. I was persuasive with them, and I had help — help that spit lead hundreds of metres per second. The restaurant I drove to was Paolo's office. All the city's underworld business ran through the building like blood through a hard corrupted heart. Paolo wanted to see me one last time before he killed me. Paolo had sent me on a job. I stole evidence for him that would wipe the competing mob, the Russians, off the map in Hamilton. What Paolo never told me was that it was also my job to lead the Russians away from him. Paolo wanted them to chase me while he put the final nails in their coffins. It would have worked too. Next to no one knew I worked for Paolo. No one outside of a handful of people knew I even existed. I was an apparition in the city — someone who did jobs quietly. Jobs a man like Paolo would want to distance himself from. I had been used by

Paolo, but instead of laying down to die I went on the offensive and stayed alive. I crossed Paolo for the second time — the last time. The restaurant turned into a slaughterhouse. The Russians figured out that I worked for Paolo and they brazenly attacked the restaurant in broad daylight. A death squad showed up to hit Paolo and me at once, but nothing ever goes according to plan in this city. The Russians couldn't finish the job. Paolo and I survived although we were both a few ounces of lead heavier.

After leaving Paolo and the Russians on the floor of his restaurant, I drove myself to a veterinarian in the sticks. The vet was a large animal doctor who lost her family and then hit the bottle. She was unlicensed, but her work was still good and she would do it quietly for cash. I was sure that no one from Paolo's crew or the Russian mob could have heard of her.

I made it to her house and parked out back. I staggered to her door with a brick of cash in my right hand, and used the solid rectangle of money to hammer on the door. I waited in the dim light for a minute until a porch bulb spontaneously combusted into light above my head. The bright light and blood loss made me dizzy; the glow also called out to every insect on the ten-acre property. Mosquitoes and horseflies circled my body on their way to the bulb, causing me to stumble as I swatted the insects buzzing in my ears with the only arm I could use. I swatted at the flies like King Kong swatted at airplanes. My attacks were less balanced than the huge ape's, and I had to give up and use my good arm to balance myself. I pushed the brick of cash the door frame with my right hand and braced myself for another insect barrage.

The door was flung open and, in shadows behind the porch light, a woman stood holding a large plastic cup in her hands.

MIKE KNOWLES

"Hep you?" The "L" in "help" was slurred out by whatever she was drinking from the cup.

"I need medical attention."

"You're not a . . . not a horse. Heh. Do you know that? You're not a horse."

I risked losing my balance again and held the brick of cash out. "I know I'm not a horse, but technically you're not a vet. I know you work freelance . . . and I know your fee."

She stared at the money and licked her lips. "How much is it?"

"Ten," I said. "You get another five when I walk out of here."

"Who told you 'bout me?" she asked.

"Some Irish guys told me you were good and private."

"Ten now. Five later?"

"Five when I walk out of here," I corrected.

"How do I know you'll pay?" she asked, not drunk enough to miss that part of the deal.

"You don't, but the ten up front should be enough to get me a tab."

She thought about it for a minute. "What's your name?"

"Call me Mr. Ed."

She laughed her way into a coughing fit, wiped her chin on the neck of her shirt, and then led me into the house. I spent a week and a half in my drunken doctor's care until I was able to leave upright and mobile. The bullet in the back of my arm was out, and the painkillers she gave me worked fine. I paid her as promised and drove back into the city. I had to tie up some loose ends before I left for good.

I didn't have a life on the grid. Nothing was in my name directly — everything was layered. The layers kept me apart from everyone and everything. I spent my youth training and learning to live a life of discipline and paranoia. If I was going to get killed, it was never going to be because some-one tracked me down through the system. The only point of contact between me and the circles I moved in was the office. The office was clean save a few items that were important but disposable. There were guns that needed to be lost in a place no one would ever find them. The guns weren't traceable to me, but they had a history that could be tied to the fingerprints that were all over the room. The office also had money hidden inside which, in my current situation, had to also be considered disposable. I wasn't going back to the office — not ever — but I needed it cleaned out.

I pulled the car up to a curb outside a row of mailboxes at a plaza on Main Street. The street ran through Hamilton into the smaller suburbs of Dundas and Stoney Creek. The plaza in Dundas was busy from nine in the morning to ten at night with people shopping, eating, bowling, or getting haircuts. I got out of the car and did a little of everything, to blend in and watch for a tail. I picked up a few items and walked with my bags into the post office. I produced a key from my key ring and opened box 113. The box looked as empty as usual, but it didn't matter. I reached my hand in and pulled at another box inside. The second container was painted the same colour as the brown interior of the mail-box and had a finger hole drilled into it so that it could be slid out. I had to lean back hard to move the tiny box with my one good arm. All at once my weight dislodged the powerful magnets I put inside. I excused myself to the woman I stepped back into, and put the box into my shop-ping bag. The box was still as heavy as I had left it — a fact that brought a grin to my face.

I performed the same routine at seven other plazas out-side Hamilton. Each of the mailboxes contained a similar hidden box, and each was untouched since I had left it.

Each box contained a brick of cash composed of the same large-denomination bills. In total, I collected two hundred thousand, twenty-five from each box.

My next stop was an Internet café. It was a busy shop bustling with Asian exchange students and employees from the tattoo parlour and coffee shop located on either side of the café. I logged into a local bank account I set up in a name that had nothing to do with me, and checked the balance. I had six thousand forty-three dollars and change. I closed the screen and opened up a search engine. I used the computer to find the phone numbers of the utility companies I paid monthly bills to for the house and office. On paper, the house belonged to a name my uncle created in the seventies. My uncle was a ghost in the system and his death went unnoticed by the law. I inherited the house when I burned his body and I kept the alias alive on paper. I never used the house unless I had to so the bills were never high, but they would pile up if I were gone a long time. I took one of the pens left behind at the work station, wrote the numbers I found on the Internet on a piece of paper, and logged off the computer. I paid five dollars for my time and left the café in search of a phone. I found it down the street in Jackson Square Mall. The mall had once, decades ago, been the city's premier shopping destination, but years of urban decay left it hollow and lifeless. The mall lost its trendy stores in exchange for dollar shops and discount clothing warehouses. Most of the people left after everyone of means followed the trendy stores uptown. The remaining shoppers were bored transients with no way to follow anyone anywhere.

I found a row of scarred vandalized pay phones outside a hotel that exited into the mall. I tried two phones only to find them gum-filled or mysteriously wet. The third was intact and produced a faint dial tone. I pulled the phone numbers I brought, and the pen I stole, and called each utility twice, logging the balance owed first on the house then on the office. Once I recorded each debt, I made my way back to the Internet café.

My unit was still empty so I logged on to it once again. I paid all of my bills, home and office, from two separate accounts. Once I had paid everything that was owing, I tucked the paper away and left the pen where I had found it.

I drove to the house not bothering to wind through any special routes. I was surprised at my direct approach, even more at my internal logic, which made me believe no one could have possibly been on my tail yet. I didn't feel like myself anymore. I was losing the connection to the paranoia that ran my life. It wasn't filtering my every move now; it felt more like a tiresome habit I was happy to be rid of rather than a means of keeping me alive.

I pulled into the driveway and sat behind the wheel. I hated the house. I had lived there with my uncle until it became mine following his death. My long stay started as a visit, waiting for my parents to return from a "business trip." They never came back, and as a result I was passed on to the only family I had — my uncle. He wasn't mean, he was just distant. He made me go to school, do my homework, and read. The reading wasn't solely for me; it was to give us things to talk about. The reading led to talking and the talking led to my real education. I learned how to read between the lines of books and then between the lines of conversations. Once I learned how to dissect what people said, it didn't take long for me to find out that my parents were thieves. They took jobs that were high risk and high cash. The jobs allowed them to give me a normal life in a house with friends and a school. Once I learned about them, it was an easy jump to become involved with my uncle and his "work." He was like my parents in that he wasn't honest, but unlike them in that he lived a life detached from everything — no kids, no friends, no connections to the world to speak of. It was how he survived intact long after my parents died.

I told my uncle I wanted to do what my parents did, and eventually he introduced me to the life. It wasn't my parents' life exactly — it was his. He taught me to be like him, and like Alice down the rabbit hole, I was whisked off the grid.

cleaned out the house in twenty minutes. I took the address book, money from the floorboards, and an old .38 to carry with the Glock I had on me. I unplugged everything and made a plan to mail post-dated cheques to the landscaper who cut the lawn in the summer and shovelled the driveway in the winter. He would also pick up any flyers left on the property. The rest of the junk mail would fall through the large slot in the door, leaving no evidence that the house was empty.

Before leaving the city, I stopped at a pay phone two blocks from Sully's Tavern. I called the bar and got an answer on the third ring.

"Sully's," Steve's low, calm voice answered.

"How would you like to earn ten grand with a handkerchief?"

"I was worried. I thought you went down after that business with the restaurant."

"You, worried?"

"You looked like shit the last time I saw you."

I must have been circling the drain because Steve never said he worried; he usually said nothing at all. Before I could say anything else, he spoke again. "What's this about ten thousand dollars?"

"I need you to get into the office and wipe it down top to bottom. There's forty grand in the baseboard behind my desk and a CD taped to the underside of the window ledge. Grab both when you leave, and ten of the forty is yours."

"You leaving?"

I ignored the question. "That business at the restaurant. Was it on the news?"

"Nah, just gossip."

"My name get thrown around?"

"Nah, but who else is going to start trouble there?" Steve chuckled over the background of clinking glasses and bar conversation.

"I'm leaving for a while. I just need to make sure there are no loose ends at the office."

"Why don't you burn it down?"

It was my turn to chuckle. I was amazed at how easily Steve's mind gravitated towards violence, as though it were the most logical answer and therefore the first suggestion. "There are already enough people involved. Fires bring firemen and cops; I just need to get rid of the prints and the money."

"Guns?"

"They're in a compartment in the closet; they're as safe as they'll ever be, but they need to be wiped." There was no immediate reply; I listened to the sounds of the bar for half a minute. "Steve?"

"I'll do it for free."

"Steve!" I protested.

"I'll do it for free."

I finished talking to Steve and told him I would leave

the key in the change return of the phone I was on. I thanked my friend and hung up. By the time he got to the key, I would be in the car and out of the city.

I drove eight hours to Montreal. I found a cheap motel that took cash and slept without worry for the night. I woke at eight and used a washcloth to clean everything around the bandages. The pain in my left arm was unbelievable, but the pills the vet gave me would wear it down. I found the nearest post office and mailed twelve cheques and a note to the landscaper who took care of the house. The note told him I would be away on business often over the coming year. I made sure he understood that I would be coming back home every now and again to make sure that the landscaper would not think he could get away with neglecting the lawn. I also asked him to dispose of any flyers left on the driveway or grass. I wanted no sign that the house was unoccupied. After that, I ate a huge breakfast at a French-Canadian chain that was much like Denny's except for the fact that it offered baked beans with every meal.

Full and dulled from the painkillers, I drove twelve more hours to the only other place I had ever been — Prince Edward Island.

Mom and Dad took me to the island as a boy, and together we did everything that the small island offered. It was more than a vacation; it was my only solid memory of family. I could still close my eyes and smell the water, feel the breeze, and hear the sound of the red singing sand squeaking under my feet.

My return was greeted by a monument to technological advancement. Instead of a ferry crossing, there loomed a huge bridge joining the gap between New Brunswick and Prince Edward Island. A small turn-off advertised the old ferry, but I chose the new bridge instead. I wanted to get to the island as fast as possible. The bandages on my arm were starting to feel moist under my shirt. I needed to find a place to stay so I could rest and heal.

The bridge led to Charlottetown — the capital city, as large as a small Ontario town. The roads introducing me to the island province were different than those before the bridge — their asphalt was tinged pink from the red island dirt used to build them. I pushed myself to drive the thirty minutes from the bridge to the city centre. I had no patience left in me to wait for sleep. As soon as traffic began to bunch at stoplights, I pulled into the first lobster-themed motel I saw. I paid for a week upfront in cash and walked straight towards the adjoining restaurant.

I was greeted inside the restaurant by the smell of frying seafood. The bubbling sound of the fryers muffled the eating noises of the four solitary patrons. I was too tired to attempt eating anything that would require two hands, so I ordered a bowl of fish chowder and an order of fish and chips. The chowder came fast and it was hot and creamy. I had to search for the advertised pieces of crab and lobster until I finally found a piece of each on the bottom of the bowl. The fish and chips arrived minutes later in a red plastic basket. The oily fish and fries lay atop a piece of waxed paper printed to look like old newsprint. The fish was good; it settled deep in my stomach and made me immediately bone weary. I dropped a twenty down and left the restaurant without waiting for the almost nine dollars in change I would have gotten back.

I went to my room without my bags and went to sleep on the bed. I woke fourteen hours later and spent the following week in a painkiller haze. After the seven days at the motel, I felt good enough to travel away from the city deeper into the heart of the island. An hour out of Charlottetown, I stopped at an Atlantic Superstore to look

14

at the community bulletin board, and found a house for rent minutes away from the ocean. Nellie, the old woman renting the house, was pleasant and inquisitive. She gave me directions to the house and met me there in her apron. I put her in her sixties, but her hair still had much of its youthful red. Her face was worn but tight; she was a woman who would age well until she finally could no longer age at all. Nellie fought the urge to ask questions about my long stay for fifteen whole seconds. I told her that I just had to get away from the city, and she instantly understood me as though I had just spoken some immutable truth. She told me five minutes worth of big-city horror stories that I was sure she had never learned first hand before we agreed on the evils of big cities and a price for the house. I paid her up front for four months, in cash, and she left me alone in the house holding the keys.

I hadn't lied to Nellie. I did have to get away from the city. I had made enemies of both sides of the underworld — Italian and Russian — making my presence dangerous on a good day. Add to that the condition of my mangled left arm, and I wouldn't last a day in Hamilton. I needed to start over where no one could find me. I needed to rehab my body. Most of all I needed to find a new way of life; something different from my parents' way, and most important different from my uncle's way. I needed to find a life all my own and shape it myself.

I spent days walking the long road in front of the house to the local beaches and wharves. Each day I tried to swing my left arm more and more to bring back its range of motion. After a month of walking, I could swing my arm to shoulder height making my walks awkward to look at. Once I looked sufficiently stupid swinging my arms, I switched to running in the forests that surrounded the house. I used my arms to pull myself over fallen tress and up hills. I lost my grip often and fell at least ten times a day at first, but after another month I could run for hours unimpeded.

My left arm began feeling normal, but different angles brought with them immense pain. On one of my trips into town for food, I found a gym overtop of a local hockey arena. I ran in the mornings, using the forest to bring my arm back, and used the gym in the evenings. Slowly, I began to be able to move dumbbells off my chest. It took two more months before I felt in shape. I was better, but I wasn't what I was. I knew I didn't have to be like I was anymore, but I couldn't let the wound be what changed me. The wound was like the city holding on to me — letting me know I couldn't escape. I had to get its hand off me. I doubled the workouts and used the stairs at the house to do angled one-arm push-ups. At first, the strain on my joints caused me to scream, but I built up from less than one to sets of ten. By the summer, when my seventh month at the house ended, I could do fifteen one-arm push-ups reversed on the stairs with my feet elevated above me. I pounded out rep after rep, hardly feeling the strain on my joints. It was about this time that I went stir crazy.

The small town offered little in the way of entertainment. There was a grocery store and drug store that combined also covered the town's book, hardware, and appliance needs, and a theatre that played movies already released on DVD. The only real excitement was the fishing. I loved to watch the fishermen bring in their hauls at the end of the day.

I watched in awe as boat after boat pulled in with bluefin tuna that weighed hundreds of pounds. The biggest fish were dragged in behind the boats — the carcasses staying fresh in the briny water that had given them life minutes before. The fishermen took turns raising the giant fish onto the docks. Tour groups stood with the hanging catch for photo opportunities — the captains smiling biggest of all. They got the profit of the catch while the charter passengers got the cheap photo and the priceless story to go along with it.

Once the photos were taken, the largest tuna were taken apart on the dock with a chainsaw. In the same spot in which they had just been immortalized on film forever, they were dissected for the value of their parts and put on ice. The large tuna were soon riding the ocean once more, only it was in the belly of a boat bound for Japan.

I watched the haul every day I could before making the long walk back to the house in the woods. On my way home one night, I decided I would book a charter of my own.

On a cold Wednesday morning, I headed out fishing with a man named Jeff. His boat *Wendy* was worth hundreds of thousands of dollars making me think the giant fish must be worth their weight in cash.

"Good money in this?" I asked as we plowed through the water.

"Charters? Oh, sure, couple a fellas out on the water makes me a good bit for sure," he said.

"Not the charters, the fishing. The boat doesn't look cheap."

"Fishing is a funny thing. When it's good it pays the bills and more for sure, but when it's bad you can't even put fish on the table." He laughed at his own joke for a second before going on. "Chartering is like the middle. It gives me some cash on a slow day, and if we catch something I get that too."

"Win, win," I said. Jeff smiled at me and looked out at the vast expanse of water ahead. The blowing sea air was clean; nothing polluted it with exhaust or pollen. I breathed deep as though for the first time and smiled. It wasn't the cold grin I learned from my uncle that usually came before violence — it was a genuine smile. I was happy on the water.

Once we came to a stop in the water, Jeff pulled a fish from a tub at the back of the boat; it wriggled alive in his hands.

"If this is your idea of fishing, I want my money back."

"Get lost, boy. This is the bait. The fish love 'em. But first . . ." He put the fish down on a work table and pulled a knife from a magnetic strip that held it above the work surface. He cut the fish into chunks and threw the pieces into a stained bucket. He repeated the process, pulling more fish from the tub to chunk them on the table.

"Why not just do this ahead of time."

"You gotta do it this way. The tuna like it fresh, and if the bait is too cold they'll spit it out before the hook gets in."

"They can spit?" I said. My tone gave away the fact that I thought I was being fed a script meant to entice the tourists.

Jeff stopped his bloody work and looked me in the eye. He pointed at me with the knife, and his words had no humour in them. "You got to get your head around what you're dealing with here. These aren't goldfish you're hunting. These are monsters. Dangerous monsters who know what they like, and aren't afraid to tell you different."

I nodded at the knife and realized Jeff didn't work from a script. "How do you know there are tuna here?" I asked.

"I work this water every day. I know where the monsters are, but you can check the fish finder if you don't believe me, city boy."

I followed his directions up the stairs to the fish finder beside the wheel of the boat. The screen showed a scattering of yellow dots; below the yellow spatter were two large red dots. "What am I looking at?" I yelled back to Jeff.

"The yellow dots are a school of mackerel. Those fishes are running for their lives down there for sure."

I walked back down the stairs to find Jeff looking over the side of the boat at the dark water. "Are the red dots tuna then?"

He smiled at me and put one gloved finger to his nose, closing a nostril. He pushed air hard through his nose, shooting snot over the side. "Those red dots, city boy, are giant bluefin tuna. Not your canned tuna. Big fuckin' monsters for those Japanese fellows to have with rice and sake. Godzillas with gills, for sure."

"How big?"

"Anywhere between two hundred and a thousand pounds. I told you it's no goldfish; it's a bull. It runs fast and it doesn't get tired. This thing will fight you like nothing else."

"How do we catch it?"

"You stand over there and you hold that rod tight. You paid for the experience so you can go mano-a-fisho for a little while. You can let it beat your ass until you're ready to hand it over."

I put a hand on the pole and watched the water lap the boat while Jeff threw bait over the side. The chunks sank fast, leaving no trace they ever existed until Jeff threw more on top of them.

"I want the fish to swim figure eights around the boat. If he's into the bait he'll stick around for more."

On the third toss, I saw a dark shape streak by the boat under the splash of the raw fish. Jeff saw the streak and laughed under his breath. He baited the large metal hook with something white before spearing a large chunk of bait.

"What is the white stuff?"

"Styrofoam, city boy; it came with the new TV. The

hook is heavy. The foam gives it a bit of lift so it won't sink before Godzilla gets a chance to pass it by. Secure the pole, city boy."

I grabbed the pole, anchored in the metal holster, with two hands while Jeff threw the baited hook over. Even though the pole was propped up by the holster, I could still feel its heavy weight; it was nothing like the fibreglass rods I used as a kid. I breathed deep and cleared my mind while I waited for the giant below to grab the loaded bait. Jeff and I sat quiet in the boat. No more questions or sarcastic remarks passed between us. I stared at the line, happy for the calm minutes on the ocean. As if the giant below sensed my happiness, the line began to run out, yard after yard, away from the *Wendy*.

"He can run fast and deep for almost three hundred yards. Problem is he swims with his mouth closed. Eventually he's gonna have to slow down to open his mouth and breathe."

The line ran from the pole as though I had shot something into the water, the reel releasing its heavy line as though there were no drag at all. After a long minute, the rapidly fleeing line began to slow, and that's when the real fight began. I stood, heaving against the rod, for what felt like hours. I followed every instruction the suddenly serious captain gave me. Jeff never asked me to turn over the pole; he just guided me in killing the giant.

After an hour of endless fighting, I began to see the head of my foe. My left arm burned with the effort of fighting the bluefin, but I never let go. I was up against my first real test and I was not going to blink. Little by little I began to see more of the head of my enemy; it was heavy and fierce, its eyes alive with fear and the marine equivalent of adrenaline.

As I dragged the fish closer and closer to the boat, Jeff

stopped watching me with his hawk eyes and turned to retrieve a huge pole off the a rack at from the stern. The pole was old and worn and had a large black hook on the end. The tool didn't match the many technological advancements on the boat — it was a relic from harder times. It was a grim instrument, one I later learned to call a gaff, and it made the tuna's tremendous opposition all at once understandable.

"Bring it closer," he yelled.

I manoeuvred the tuna beside the boat, and Jeff bent over the side and swung the hook into the flesh behind the head of the bluefin tuna. With my help, he dragged the fish into the boat. It hit the deck with a thud and helplessly slapped its tail against the deck as though it were only air-borne and not helplessly dying. I felt a pang of empathy for the fish. I knew what it was to be beaten to the point of death.

If Jeff caught my expression he didn't show it; he just looked over the fish and then at his watch. "We got time to get this back in before it starts to spoil. If we stay out I have to bleed it and pack it with ice. That would take about as long as it would take us to just cruise into the dock."

"How big is it?" I asked.

"'Bout three hundred pounds, city boy."

"How long would it take for one of the real big fish?"

"That's five or six hours of hard work, but it's easier at the end. We don't bring them into the boat when they're that big. We secure them by the tail and tow 'em in to be lifted out with a small crane."

"So you get all the cash for this catch plus what I paid?"

Jeff smiled at me. "Sometimes it pays to be an island fisherman, eh, city boy? But it ain't all easy. No, I gotta haul it in, get it ready with the saw, and then clean up the boat. No, the job ain't all roses, that's for sure."

"Sounds like you need help."

"Had a college kid, but he quit on me. Thought the hours were too long. Ha, I told him you want to make a living on the boat you gotta be out before the sun and you only stop when it's long gone. There's lots of island kids looking for work. I'll take another on before long and work him till he decides he's meant for other things. Kids today don't want to work all day fighting the fish; it's easier to go work at Subway. There the only fish you fight are already at the bottom of a bucket."

I thought about it for a minute — the minute was fifty-nine more seconds than I needed. In the last four hours, I hadn't thought about home or my arm once. "I want to work for you, Jeff," I said.

"Why's a city boy want to get his hands dirty for peanuts? 'Cause make no mistake, that's what I pay. I don't share the profits."

I used the same excuse I'd given Nellie. "I need to get away from the city."

Jeff smiled again. My answer seemed to be some secret code that everyone on the island silently understood. "Well," he said, gesturing at the expanse of ocean, "ya won't get much farther away than this."

CHAPTER **FOUR**

spent the rest of the season searching for giants with my captain. I was paid a low hourly wage, and I was treated better — he didn't talk to me like I was an idiot more than three times an hour. I learned the ins and outs of fishing off the coast and in the deep ocean. Because I wasn't paying anymore, I was no longer the one holding the rod. Jeff fought the monsters while I followed orders. Between bouts of frantic reeling, he explained how to sense when to pull and when to let the fish run. The only job left for me was gaffing. Once the fish was close enough to see the panic in its lidless eyes, it was my job to bury the hook behind its thrashing head. The trick was timing the strike so that the gaff sunk deep into shoulder of the fish. The shoulder was dense enough to support the weight of the fish as it was pulled from the water and it was far away from the prime meat. After a few weeks at sea, I could bury the hook deep in the fish without a moment's hesitation. It was like stabbing a person up close. All at once, the panicked eyes went even wilder until they dulled as the fish resigned itself to its fate. If the fish was big enough, I was demoted to harpooner. I would spear the fish, to bring it closer to death and even closer to the gaff. When the true monsters were circling the drain, we hooked them with wire and dragged their carcasses back to port. The part of me that felt remorse for the first fish I saw dragged into the boat vanished after my second trip out. Part of me, a part I tried to pretend was gone, enjoyed the thrill of the fight. It wasn't the cruelty that brought me back day after day. It was the skill of the hunt and the artistry of the perfect blow with the gaff. Fishing felt like reflex. I used the old muscles I had developed working with my uncle and for Paolo Donati. As much as I thought I wanted a new life, there were some things I couldn't unlearn, even out on the ocean away from all the city lights and smells.

At the end of the fishing season, Jeff went on EI, even though he had earned almost six figures from the tuna and charters. I spent the winter in the house . . . working out and having a nightly meal with my captain and his wife Wendy. Each night, I was invited back into Jeff's home and treated as though I were a member of the family rather than an employee. My awkwardness and lack of social skills wore off fast in the loving home. I learned to enjoy dinner, and began to look forward to it. Soon I found myself keeping tabs on interesting things to bring up over dinner. The dinners expanded to weekends. I watched movies with Jeff and spent time admiring his hunting rifles while I was told stories about the ones that got away. Through all the stories and firearm showcasing, I played ignorant pretending to be in awe of the dangerous weapons.

I loved my new friends. A fact which made it hard to hide what I was. We spoke mainly about fishing and life on the island. When I was put on the spot about my life before the island, I stuck to generic comments and terms

24

like "rat race," which got me appreciative nods. So long as I spoke of the city in clichés, I was safe from further probing — even safer from losing my new friends. My old life was something few would be able to understand, and a good man like Jeff would never allow me to be near his wife and business if he knew what I was. I understood this — he had priorities and they were sacred to him. I was still searching for my own new priorities, and for a while I thought the search was narrowing as I began to truly become a part of other people's lives again for the first time since my parents died. I laughed and smiled more often; I even forgot to check over my shoulder once in a while. The island had healed my body, but it had trouble healing the rest of me.

The winter ended, and we went back on the boat. I was strong and healthy, but tired. I was sleeping less and less with each night on the island. My first nights in my new home had been long and restful, but each passing day took with it precious minutes. I collapsed into an ever shortening dreamless sleep each night waking before the sun in the loud silence of the house.

Together Jeff and I fished and worked charter groups of die-hard anglers out for a new challenge and loud drunken businessmen taking days away from the difficult island golf courses. After each day of fishing, Jeff would take the charter off the boat with the catch and set up for a photo. The people who had chartered the boat crowded together to get in the shot while I stayed clear. Jeff had stopped trying to include me, deciding it was a fight he would never win; he left me to clean the boat while he schmoozed the clients for the last few minutes. I stayed clear of the crowds and their cameras despite the fact that I hadn't been anywhere close to trouble for almost two years. Part of me couldn't let go of all of the years of training beaten into me by my uncle. While I stopped looking over my shoulder all of the time, I couldn't let myself be captured on film for anyone to see. I was happy to clean the blood off the boat and prepare for the following day. Life went like this for months until the day I slipped up and was caught off guard.

Four politicians down from Ottawa caught an eight-hundred-pound bluefin at the tail end of a slow day. I was cleaning up the boat while they took their picture and quietly conversed around the hanging fish when one of the men grabbed his chest and uttered that he was having chest pains. His friends searched his pockets for his pills, but they were in his bag — left behind on the boat with me. Jeff yelled for me to bring down the bag and I did it without thinking. I ran as my right hand searched the bag for the pills. I had them in my hand as I reached the crowd of people around the man, who was lying on the dock. I didn't check to see what kind of safety top was on the pill bottle; I just dug a nail into the plastic and sent a geyser of white pills flying over the dock. I dug one of the remaining pills out of the container and tried to shove it down the man's throat, but he was too far gone. He died on the dock, below the massive fish he helped pull in. Camera flashes pelted the body from nosy tourists who took shots of the scene before I could move out of the way. One of the shots, one with a profile of my face as I bent down to help the dying man, got national coverage in the papers. The man who died was a politician who was pro big business and against protecting Canada's national resources. Headlines like "Nature Fights Back" led the picture out to the rest of the country. I saw the photo the next day after Jeff slapped the newspaper on the back of my head.

"Ya managed to get your ugly face into the paper. Well, half of it anyway, didn't ya, city boy? Yer just lucky my face was in it to balance it out. Yer mug would scare off the tourists."

I ignored the comment as I looked at my face created out of thousands of meticulously placed ink dots. My face had been sent out across the country for everyone to see. It was that front page postcard that brought the man to the wharf; he was there because of the picture. He was there for me.

Few people came to the wharf alone, and no one did it dressed like he was going to a club. The outsider was not dressed to fish or tour — he had no camera, fishing pole, or binoculars. He didn't even seem to be interested in the large fish being cut to pieces by the chainsaw. He just stood at the edge of the pier watching people get into their cars. I pulled my hat down low and bent over pretending to work around the boat. I thought I had an agreement with my old boss, Paolo Donati, and his criminal army. After I helped Paolo survive his very own Russian revolution, he said we were even. The man on the wharf said different.

I closed my eyes and thought about the photo. I stared at it when I first saw it — enraged at my stupidity. I got too comfortable and I paid for it. The picture had my face in it and the boat's name was in the caption. Soon the guy with the pointy shoes would get tired of waiting and watching the wrong people walk by. He would get impatient and decide to walk around the ships looking for the boat named "Wendy." It was close to the end of the day, the perfect time for someone looking to go unnoticed to walk down to the boats. People were coming and going all over the pier; no one would pay much attention to an out-of-place man looking at the ships

I moved to the other side of the boat and took a seat. If I finished the nightly cleanup, there would be no reason for me to stay on board. I wanted to be the only one around when Pointy Shoes came looking for me. I wanted him to be out of his element when he made his play, so I had to wait and make sure Jeff couldn't see me taking it easy while he schmoozed on the dock with the day's charter.

I got up twenty minutes later after feeling the boat slightly shift with the addition of my captain's weight. I scanned the wharf, noticing how empty it had become. There were a few fisherman left hosing off their boats and loading their trucks, and one other man still watching the parking lot.

"Shit, city boy. You're not done yet? I'll help ya get finished, 'cause at this pace you'll be here all night."

"Sorry, Jeff. I just got to thinking and it slowed me down. You don't need to stick around. I'll finish up here. You get home to Wendy; she's probably craving something."

"Don't ya know, that is for sure. Her and that baby have me going everywhere for food. The only thing she doesn't crave is tuna. At least I could bring that home with me. Last night I had to go into Charlottetown for Taco Bell. I wasn't in bed until one." He sighed and looked around at the mess on the boat. "Make sure to lock her up when you're done, city boy."

"Tell Wendy I said hey."

"Tell her yourself at dinner. After you're done here."

The rest of his goodbyes trailed off as he walked away from the boat. I watched him go, making sure to stand straight up on the side of the boat so I could be seen from the parking lot. I watched Jeff pass Pointy Shoes; they nodded a greeting to one another as Jeff walked over to his car. Pointy Shoes pulled a piece of paper from his pocket and unfolded it. I guessed it was the newspaper photo. He glanced at the paper, then turned to look at Jeff again.

MIKE KNOWLES

While his back was to me, I took off my hat. When his head turned back, I made an elaborate production of stretching and wiping my forehead. I didn't look in the direction of Pointy Shoes, but I was sure he was looking at me. I walked to the ladder on the side of the boat while, in my peripheral vision, I watched my audience consult his piece of paper once again. He was comparing me to the paper. I made my way down the ladder to the dock. Once I had two feet on the wood planks, I kneeled at the ropes holding the boat to the dock. I untied one of the knots and began retying it slowly. With my right hand, I unsheathed the knife I kept at the small of my back. The knife was a worn fishing knife that I used everyday; it was battered, but razor sharp. Jeff always made fun of the way I carried my knife, but I could never force myself to wear it out in the open or leave it in a pocket where it was hard to pull free. A concealed weapon always felt more natural.

I put the knife on the dock beside my foot, so that it was hidden from anyone approaching. I flipped one loose end of the rope over one side of the knot then the other, pretending to be unsure about the right way to finish. I didn't have to pretend long before I heard the squeak of old worn wood planks groaning under human weight. Pointy Shoes was walking towards me. Being on my knees made me an obvious target. Every schoolyard bully loved to shove a kid when he was down on a knee tying his shoe. Pointy Shoes was just a bigger schoolyard bully — one with a paycheque.

I looked in his direction as he approached, smiled, and said, "Evening." Looking at him to say hello let me see that his hands were empty. A fact that made me happy.

He didn't smile back; he just stopped eight feet away and spread his feet apart. I didn't want to act first because there was still a small chance that this guy was a tourist or maybe just a reporter doing a follow-up story. "You want to book a charter, you'll have to talk to the boss. I can give you his number if you want, or you can come back tomorrow."

I got no response at first from the man with the pointy shoes. I looked into his eyes and I knew there was no way he was a tourist or even a reporter. His greeting relieved all lingering doubts about what he really was.

"Hey, Wilson."

I remained on my knees as our eyes locked. My face didn't register surprise, instead it pulled into an expression I thought I had forgotten. My face made an ugly grin, my uncle's grin. It was a look that I learned the hard way. Whenever I thought I knew the score, I would see the look on my uncle's face and know I was wrong. The look tormented me, but I was lucky — everyone else who saw it usually wound up dead. I spent years learning my uncle's craft, years surviving his tutelage, until the same grin became my property. Pointy Shoes saw it and it told him something he didn't like. It said I wasn't afraid. It said I wasn't even surprised. It said I knew something he didn't. My grin said all of this in a fraction of a second.

Pointy Shoes was good; he didn't waste time looking confused. He instead reached behind his back under the stretchy fabric of his synthetic shirt. His reaction didn't faze me; I was good too, better than this guy, even after two years of rusting. My right hand found the knife by my foot, and I lobbed it in the direction of Pointy Shoes. The throw was slow and sloppy not because I was rusty, but rather because I wanted Pointy Shoes to use both of his hands. He gave up on whatever was behind his back and decided to try to catch the slowly spinning knife moving towards his chest.

Instinct is a funny thing; every person will always opt to save himself over almost any other choice. It takes years of training and experience to be able to fight the primal urge for self-preservation. Pointy Shoes chose personal safety over inflicting harm on me. He didn't catch the knife; he only managed to knock it out of the air. Pointy Shoes let out a sigh of relief just before my fist crushed his collar bone like a beer can. The blow knocked the air out of him, pushing with it any means of screaming. To his credit, Pointy Shoes stayed standing; he just crumpled inward like he was a balloon losing air. My heavy work boot smashed his instep knocking him off balance and into my hands. The fishing and rehabilitation had turned my grip into something close to a vise. His greasy hair had nowhere to go in my hands but down, dragging his face to my rising knee. Pointy Shoes fell to the old salt-soaked boards as though he were poured from a cup. His body just splashed unconscious at my feet. The few leftover fishermen were too far away to see what had just happened in four seconds beside the *Wendy*, and the sound couldn't have carried over the roar of motors and lapping water.

I bent down and loosened the rest of the ropes holding the boat to the dock. Once the boat was free, I pulled Pointy Shoes into a fireman's carry. I laughed to myself when I realized that holding a full-grown man on my shoulders and climbing a ladder onto a boat were close to effortless. I had healed in time.

I put Pointy Shoes in the bow and went to the wheel to fire up the diesel engine. The engine roared to life and let off a cloud of smoke that I secretly inhaled every day as though it were the scent of a rare rose. The exhaust gave me something that the clean sea air never could. As time went on the smell of man-made pollution was something I craved, something I welcomed like a secret devil.

The rumbling of the engine pushed the boat through the cloud of smoke and away from the wharf. The motion of the boat caused Pointy Shoes to stir. I aimed the boat straight out to sea and walked out to meet my new friend.

Before saying hello again, I took a nickel-plated .32 Smith & Wesson revolver from Pointy Shoes's waistband along with a wallet, keys, and a cell phone from his pockets. Pointy Shoes had a name: Johnny Romeo. The name told me everything. Someone had reached out to me. Someone who should have known better.

Johnny was too out of it to cause trouble, so I went back to the wheel and guided us through the rapidly dimming light to a spot on the water where I could barely make out the lights from the dock. I yelled to Johnny as soon as I cut the engine. "What does Paolo want? Payback?"

Johnny groaned in response. He had managed to pull himself up to a sitting position against the side of the boat. His synthetic shirt had a sharp angular bulge near his neck. The unnatural distension was surrounded by a growing wetness. Johnny had a compound fracture and probably a concussion from my knee. I picked up a bucket and got water from the bait tank. The fish inside swam happily when they realized I only wanted some of their real estate.

The salt water hit him, soaking his shirt and sending pain through the wound; he sobered instantly.

"What does Paolo want, Johnny?"

"He . . . he wants to see you."

I was surprised at the answer, but I didn't dwell on it. "Why did he send you and your gun? Was that supposed to lead the way?"

"Fuck, I can't move my arm. Fuck, it hurts. I think I'm gonna be sick."

I hit him with another bucket of fish water just to keep him in the here and now.

"Jesus, he . . . he just wanted me to find you and make sure you went to see him."

MIKE KNOWLES

"He here now? On the island?"

"He's back in Hamilton at the restaurant." Johnny barely got his words out before he was sick all over himself.

"How were you going to make me go to him? Were you going to threaten me? Or were you going to force me with your shiny gun?"

Johnny looked away from me and the mess on his synthetic shirt. I read the body language and knew that he had already made a play. "What did you do, Johnny?"

He didn't answer me. He looked into my eyes and I saw that he was an errand boy. He was a hard young man who got cocky, wanted to impress his boss, and had ended up neck deep in trouble.

"You have to go meet the boss."

"Or what, Johnny? What did you do?"

"Heh, I found you yesterday and before I came down to the wharf I had tea with the nice lady who you rent from. Me and her talked all about you. Her mysterious stranger, she calls you. Can you believe that shit? The mysterious stranger who always says hello and pays his rent on time." He burped up some vomit after his last revelation.

"Where is she?"

"Don't worry about her, you got bigger problems. You need to get home."

"Where is she?"

"Fuck you."

I turned and walked back to the wheel. The diesel engine sputtered back to life, violently sending fumes in waves out over the water. I breathed the smoke in deep and felt it burn my nose as I exhaled. Each second I smelled the exhaust pulled away months of the atrophy that had set in from safe living and honest work. Almost at once, fishing with Jeff seemed years ago. I turned the boat around towards the docks and set the throttle to a slow chug. Johnny had managed to get to his feet, but the effort along with the compound fracture caused him to vomit and retch over the side. I retrieved the heavy black gaff Jeff and I used to hook the giant bluefin. The gaff was four feet long and heavy. Its hook was dulled with age, but it would still be sharp enough. The tool hung low in my hands as I walked back to Johnny who was still bent over the side of the boat.

Johnny had just finished another retch and shudder into the dark water. He turned his head in time to see me coming with the gaff in my hands. He tried to turn his body, but my left hand found the back of his neck. My hand held him in place, his chest forced against the railing. I hooked the gaff into his stomach and pulled hard towards me with my right hand. The hook moved through the synthetic shirt like it wasn't there and buried itself in Johnny's guts.

Johnny let out a scream on the desolate water, but the only person who could hear it didn't care. My left hand let go of Johnny's neck and found a metal-studded belt under his ruined shirt; I used it to propel Johnny over the side of the boat into the water. All of the noises Johnny made were eaten by the merciless ocean. I gripped the railing hard with one hand and held tight to the gaff towing Johnny's body through the water. I clenched my jaw shut and held tight as the veins in my forearm began to stand out. Johnny was dragged through the wake of the boat backwards by the gaff. The speed of the water and the weight of his body made sure that the hook wouldn't dislodge. I braced myself and held the gaff at an angle that allowed Johnny's head to stay above the water so he wouldn't die on me right away. His flailing arms and legs created a lot of drag, making his body feel as though it weighed a ton.

After a minute, I pulled Johnny up into the boat by the

gaff. He coughed up sea water from his lungs and communicated his agony is low groans. He lay face down on the deck of the *Wendy*, impaled on the gaff. The hook was buried deep in his belly, making the wooden handle stand straight up in the air like a fence post. Johnny lay still while I caught my breath, watching the lights of the docks off in the distance. We were moving so slowly that it seemed the lights were no closer than when I had turned the boat around.

"See, Johnny, this is how we bring the big tuna in once we catch them. We drag them behind the boat until all of the fight in them is gone. Thing is, fish like the water so they can hold on for a long while even on the end of a hook. How long you think you can stay alive in the water on the end of a big hook? Think you're tougher than a fish?"

Johnny had no response for me. His back rose and fell as he took in shallow breaths letting me know he was still alive. "I want to know what you did to the old lady, Johnny. You keep me in the dark much longer and I'll show you how much a fish has to put up with. I'll drag you the rest of the way back so I can get a hold of the chainsaw they use on the dock. You saw them do that today, didn't you? It'll be much easier with you. I promise."

Johnny's eyes fluttered and opened; his lips began to form a word over and over again. I put my hands on the gaff and pulled, lifting Johnny off the deck of the boat. If you ignored the hook in his belly, it would have looked as though he were levitating in a magic show.

"Trunk." Johnny's lips finally found a voice two feet in the air.

"She's in the trunk, Johnny?"

"Trunk. No more. Trunk." His voice was quiet and gravelly, but understandable.

The magic show continued as I pulled Johnny higher off

the deck. I muscled him over the side as he continued to groan his new mantra, "No more. Trunk. No more." His body splashed on the water and disappeared as the waves erased his existence. His hands stayed visible above the water in the boat lights, groping for something to hold on to — something that wasn't there. I breathed hard from the exertion and wiped my face with the arm of my shirt. It was then that I noticed my face. For a second time, my face had stretched into that grin I had shelved so long ago after leaving the city. It wasn't a sadist's smile; I took no pleasure in what I had done to Johnny. It was the smile of someone welcoming back an old friend. I knew then that Johnny was wrong — there was going to be more. Much more.

CHAPTER FIVE

I used the bucket to wash the blood off the deck. After three buckets of water, no one would ever know about what took place on *Wendy* after her captain went home for the night. I pushed the engine of the clean ship harder and drove the boat fast through the waves, feeling each impact like a punch. I made it back to the dock in under ten minutes. I collected Johnny's belongings tucking his gun into the waistband under the front of my shirt — the back already taken by my knife. I pocketed his phone and wallet, but kept the car keys in hand. I left the boat keys in the ignition for Jeff to find and tied off on the dock before making my way to the parking lot.

There were only two cars left in the parking lot — mine and a black Lexus. I used Johnny's key fob to pop the trunk as I approached. Inside, I saw the body of my landlady bound with duct tape. Nellie lay still in the trunk, but her rapidly blinking eyes told me she was alive. Her eyes registered fear when they adjusted to the new light from the parking lot and saw me standing over her, and panic when she saw me pull my knife. I cut the tape on her hands and feet leaving her to handle the strip on her mouth.

"Mr. Wilson! There was a man. He grabbed me and tied me up. He said he was looking for you."

I admired the steel in the old girl. She didn't cry. She kept her wits about her despite just being let out of a trunk.

"That man, he . . ."

"He's gone," I said.

"You mean you . . . you . . ."

"I mean he's gone. Now let's get you home."

I drove, and except for her directions, there was silence in the car. When I pulled into her driveway, I spoke up, putting an end to the quiet. "I'm sorry for what happened," I said.

"Why did he do that to me?"

"He needed me to do something. He took you to make sure I would do it."

"He was just so rough."

"He wouldn't have hurt you," I lied.

She paused and considered my lie before asking a question in a low voice. "What did he want?"

"It doesn't matter now," I said, ending that line of questioning. The answer seemed to satisfy her, and she opened the car door with a shaky hand.

"Goodbye, Mr. Wilson."

I said goodbye, then drove to the rental house. Speed limits on the rural island roads were eighty kilometres an hour; I pushed the car to one forty. I needed to clear out before Nellie decided to call the cops about tonight's activities. I figured I had half an hour until the shock wore off, and five minutes after that until her sense of civic duty kicked in. The house had been mine for close to two years, but no one would be able to tell by looking at it. In the kitchen sink were the spoon, fork, and pot that I used for every meal. There were a few books and magazines in the small living room and a gym bag on the floor of the bedroom I slept in. I picked up the books as I walked through the living room and dropped them in the gym bag. Then I lifted the mattress and collected the even stacks of bills that were distributed across the expanse of the box spring.

I had spent little of the money on the island. The cash paid for food, rent, and incidentals, and could not be traced to me. I had worked hard to keep myself off the grid of the small town. There were only three people on the island who knew where to find me, until today. Now, Paolo knew where I lived making the house, and the island, as safe as a burning building. Worse, Jeff's wife, his business, everything he had was at risk too. They would become chess pieces in a madman's game if I didn't knock over the board. I loaded the bag with the rest of my belongings and stopped to use the bathroom. I scanned the house over one last time as I moved towards the door. In the kitchen, I pulled the house keys from my key ring and left them on the counter before walking out of the house for the last time.

In an hour I was at the bridge, in line to get off the island. The bridge was a provincially funded con. It had cost nothing to enter the province from New Brunswick, and $27.50 to leave. There was no way out that didn't involve a wallet. The government was still the best thief I knew. The visit from Johnny and getting swindled by the province ruined my second experience with the bridge.

I drove the Trans-Canada Highway through New Brunswick at 130 kilometres an hour. I wanted to drive straight through to Hamilton, but I knew the day's work combined with the evening's action would anesthetize me before I got out of the province. I had put two more hours between me and the bridge when Johnny's cell phone started to ring. I had left the phone and wallet out on the passenger seat, so I barely had to take my eyes off the road while I picked the phone up and debated answering the call. Paolo sent Johnny to me, and if Johnny didn't answer his phone it wouldn't take Paolo long to piece together what had gone down.

I opened the phone and answered, "Yeah?"

"Is everything set up?" It was Paolo's voice riding the digital signal from Hamilton to me in the car. "You hear me, Johnny? Did you do what I told you to do?"

"I told you not to come looking for me, Paolo."

There was a ten-second pause before Paolo's voice crossed the country into my ear. "*Figlio,* I need to see you. I need your help."

"I can't help you, Paolo. You said it yourself — I'm a crow. I turned on my own, remember."

Just days before I drove to the island, I had been working for Paolo Donati — the man who ruled the Italian mob in Hamilton. I wasn't Italian, just some kind of mutt with ancestors all over parts of Europe. This made me automatically distrusted by every one of Paolo's crews. The distrust was intensified by my total lack of an identity. No one knew me so no one could vouch for me. I grew up invisible and worked with other invisible pros on all kinds of jobs. My only tie to anyone had been through blood. My uncle and I worked together; he provided the jobs through the contacts he had. Our last job was for Paolo, personally, off the books. My uncle ended up dead and I ended up unemployed. I was invisible, with no connections to any world, legal or otherwise. Paolo knew this and decided that he would use me personally for jobs he needed to distance himself from. I worked against Paolo's enemies whether they were Russians, the cops, or even his own people. No one who saw me would think I worked for a man like Paolo — a fact that made me even more useful. Over the years, I earned Paolo's trust, and eventually the hatred of everyone in his organization. Those who knew I existed saw me as an insult to everything their organization stood for. I wasn't family so I should never have been involved with jobs that should have been left to important made men. But Paolo was different from his underlings. He was unconventional as a leader, and as a result, he was more successful than any of his predecessors. He was educated and loved to muse about the nature of animals. He compared those around him to the beasts of the jungle, showing everyone how short the trip was from jungle to pavement. Better than his knowledge of animals and human nature was Paolo's understanding of the underworld he ruled. He knew how to use the mob and its rules, and more important, he knew how, and when, to circumvent them. He kept me in the fold, under wraps from his subordinates, because I did things that helped him maintain his position as king of the jungle. He believed he had me under control because I was alone and without support. He had no idea that I lived the way I had been trained. I was disconnected and solitary by choice because it made me untouchable. I was invulnerable so long as I controlled every situation by anticipating everyone's next moves. I stayed one step ahead of everyone, and survived in the most inhospitable environment. Everything I did was calculated and covert until my friendship with Steve challenged that.

Without any conscious effort, I had formed a bond with a local bar owner and his wife. Steve and Sandra were my friends — the only human contact I had. One of Paolo's men, Tommy Talarese, tried to destroy their lives, and in doing so set in motion a chain of events that rocked the underbelly of the city. Tommy Talarese wanted to show his kid how to collect protection like a man, after Steve had thrown Tommy's son out into the street. Tommy kidnapped Steve's wife, unleashing the bar owner like a wiry hurricane on the neighbourhood. Steve and I worked our way up the chain of local muscle to Tommy's front door. Many died getting Sandra back, including Tommy and his entire family.

I took the news to Paolo, attempting to spin the situation. Paolo, upon hearing the news, was already thinking of how to use the events to his advantage. That showed why Paolo held such a grip on the city: he would use anything to his advantage, even the death of one of his lieutenants. I convinced him of what he already decided for himself — that Tommy's death was best pinned on the city's other underworld organization, the Russians, rather than on a bartender. Paolo listened to me and did what he would have done anyway. He used Tommy's death to unite his crews to one purpose. Paolo struck out at the Russians, who were trying to take over everything Paolo had established. Paolo fired me and filed away what I did for later retribution. He told me I was a crow because they eat their own kind to protect themselves.

Less than a month later, Paolo brought me back into his employ. My second career with Paolo involved me only with his number two, Julian. I worked jobs that were more hush-hush than before and asked no questions. One of the jobs was stealing a bag from some computer nerds. The bag turned out to be full of Russian property. The Russians came after me, and I had no escape or backup from Paolo. Paolo was going to use what I stole to crush the Russians and he was going to let them kill me before he did it. The Russians were going to act as Paolo's payback for what I did to Tommy. Paolo was also using me to create confusion for the Russians, who had no idea who I worked for and no way to find out after I was dead. Once I figured out that Paolo hung me out to dry, I stole the bag back for the Russians, and they moved on the Italians first. The whole ordeal ended in blood with me in the middle. I saved Paolo's life, and told him I was out. He honoured the deal for almost two years.

"*Figlio,* forget what I said. You and me are square. I need you for a job. The kind of thing you used to do. Please, it has to be you. I'll pay you whatever you ask, just meet with me."

This was a new side of the man who had plotted to kill me. He seemed sincere in his desire to peacefully meet. He called me *figlio,* "son," trying to rebuild our bond over the phone like a horrible telephone commercial. "If you need to see me so bad, why didn't you come yourself?"

"This is a delicate situation. Leaving would attract too much suspicion," he said.

"Sending Johnny attracted suspicion," I said. My voice was cold and flat, betraying nothing.

"Why? What did he do? Where is he? I told him how I wanted this done. Put him on."

"Johnny crossed the line and he paid for it. You crossed the line too. I told you we were done. All you did today was force me to move."

There was a heavy sigh that must have come from deep down inside Paolo fifteen hundred kilometres away. "I was wrong about what I said about you. You're not a crow. You're a lioness. You know what lionesses do, *figlio?* They protect their cubs. I sent Johnny to ask nicely, and what do you do? You overreact like a hungry cat."

"The fancy punk kidnapped an old lady before he even met me. He wasn't here to talk."

Paolo laughed in my ear. "Ah, you see, I'm right. You

are a lioness. You protected your own from the jackals, didn't you? Johnny was overeager, probably angry. He knows what you did to Julian — everyone does."

I crippled Julian before I left the city. He was Paolo's number two and a hero to all of the up-and-comers. He was a vicious dinosaur who made his bones crushing other people's. "Julian and I were bound to collide one day. People aren't mad we fought, just that I won."

"They aren't mad, *figlio*; they hate you for it."

"And you want me to come back to that because you think I'm some lion?"

"Not a lion, *figlio*, a lioness — the mother. This has nothing to do with you being less than a man. No, it's because you left two of your cubs back in my jungle. Those cubs are still here nestled in their bar. I keep them safe for you. Now I need you to do something for *my* cubs. I need to see you."

"Give me a number," I said. He did, and I spoke up. "I'll tell you where and when." I closed the phone before he could argue.

I made it across the border into Quebec just as my eye-lids started to get heavy. I found a motel off the highway and paid cash for what was left of the night.

I hit the mattress and all of the trouble I had sleeping over the past months didn't touch me in the lumpy bed. I slept and dreamed for the first time in ages. I dreamed of a city awash in violence and shadows. I dreamed of it and smiled.

CHAPTER SIX

The motel alarm clock woke me before the sun and told me my eyes had been closed for four hours. The sleep felt longer; it felt like the kind of sleep you wake from to find the day half over. I showered and changed my clothes. I dug lightweight olive pants with deep pockets and a grey T-shirt from my bag. I also pulled out a thin blue shirt to go over my T-shirt. The shirt was not necessary in the early September heat, but it buttoned down the front and hung loose, making it perfect for concealing a stolen gun. I left the keys on the night table and was on the road before the water I had splashed on my face dried in my hair.

The road through Quebec was straight for hundreds of kilometres. I drove beside Johnny's powered-down cell phone thinking about home. PEI had always been the island. The rental house was just that, a house. Neither could take the place of where I had grown up invisible to everyone.

Hours after I left the motel, I found myself fighting my way through Montreal traffic. The barrage of cars felt like a scene from *Star Wars* — the one where the kid makes a run at the death star through a sky full of spaceships and laser beams. Vehicles came at me from all angles, most a high-speed blur. I was grateful when a break in the tension came in the form of a small traffic jam. As I sat in the still car, watching six construction workers watch two others work, I decided to power up the phone. It chimed to life and showed it still had half of the battery left. I dialled the number Paolo left me and was left speechless when he himself answered. Any other time I dealt with him, I had to work my way through layers of intermediaries before I could even leave a message.

"You around tomorrow?" I asked, looking at the time on the dashboard clock in the early afternoon sunlight.

"I got some things to do, but I can move them around."

"You want to see me then I name the time and the place."

"And the time is tomorrow. So where is the place, *figlio?*"

I hung up the phone without answering and powered it down. I thought back to all of the dinner-table conversations I had with my uncle. He taught me to read between the lines of books, to use the language to decode what was underneath. It wasn't long before I could do it with people. Using what they said and sometimes what they didn't to decipher what was going on under the surface. Paolo answered the phone himself and he was willing to meet whenever I wanted; he was even willing to adjust his schedule to accommodate me. This was unlike any interaction we ever had before. Paolo was the top of the food chain; he had people answering his calls so he didn't have to get his hands dirty dealing with the mundane. His people understood what he wanted and showed their capability, and worthiness of advancement, by handling the small day-to-day matters. No one was managing me. I got through on what sounded like a personal cell phone — something I never knew Paolo had. The more telling part of the call was his willingness to meet me. Out of principle, Paolo never accommodated anyone. He loved to think of himself as the king of the jungle; he saw himself elevated above all others. He would never obey someone else's schedule; it didn't fit with the personality of a methodical sociopathic kingpin. If Paolo was out to kill me, he never would have changed his methods; he would have seen that as beneath him. He wouldn't try to fool me in order to kill me; he would have kept things as they were and sent men to make it happen, more men after that if necessary. Paolo was into something deep, something big enough to change him, something he needed to see me about. He needed to influence a situation without being directly involved. Using someone who crossed him and left the city two years ago would do just that.

By four p.m., I was entering the outskirts of Toronto. I avoided the 407 highway and its camera tolls even though the road was newer and empty. I was leaving nothing to chance coming home. I was in the city by 5:30 and at a Mediterranean restaurant on Upper James Street by quarter to six. I chose to stop on the Hamilton mountain because most of the action in the city took place downtown away from the bright lights of chain stores and their younger clientele. The restaurant had a sign up that read "New Management." I figured it must have once been a lousy dive and someone must have still believed it could make a comeback. I could tell that the owner and I were the only ones who thought so when I walked through the smoke-grey glass doors into the vacant dining room.

The restaurant smelled wonderful, and I wondered what gruesome hidden secrets caused the management turnover. I took a seat in front of the dark-tinted glass so that I could see outside without being observed from the parking lot. I ordered gyros and ate them with water. The owner was pleasant and chatty, but both qualities faded as I ate in silence. The place stayed empty for the twenty minutes I ate; there were no other staff — just the owner and me. He was a short Arab man with a stubbly shaved head whose body shook from time to time with uncontrollable spasms. With each episode, he seemed to grit his teeth in an attempt to will himself to regain stillness. He was washing a plate behind the counter when I yelled out to him.

"Slow night?"

"No sir, it's off to a very good start."

I figured I was the beginning of a dinner rush in his mind. "How many do you get for dinner?"

There was a spasm then an answer. "Very many, sir."

It was clear the owner was an optimistic, glass-is-half-full sort of guy. "How many people are working with you tonight?" Optimistic owner or not, on his budget he had to be a realist.

He paused and looked away from me then down at the plate he was washing. His answer was sad, "Just me, sir."

I didn't feel bad for cracking his optimism; what he told me was good. "What's your name, pal?"

"I am Yousif, sir."

"Yousif, I think I'm going to get someone else to come down and sample some of your wonderful gyros," I said as I powered up Johnny's phone.

Yousif's optimism seemed to return; he spasmed then smiled. "Very good, sir," he said.

CHAPTER SEVEN

"Meet me on the mountain in twenty minutes."

"You said tomorrow."

"And you said your schedule was busy. You want to see me, get up to the Mandarin on Upper James. Wait outside the doors with your phone on. I'll call you when I get there."

Paolo started to reply, but it was no use. I closed the phone and powered it down. I looked out the grey windows at the Mandarin restaurant twenty-five metres across the parking lot. It was a Chinese buffet juggernaut that filled up nightly and probably managed to have a chokehold on Yousif's business. The old owner probably took his lumps from the buffet place and sold the failing business to a naïve person who thought there were many people out there who would choose straight Mediterranean cuisine over a buffet that covered each continent. Yousif was wrong, and he probably had many nights alone in his money pit to mull over his mistake. From where I sat in the empty dining room, I could watch Paolo arrive and decide whether or not I actually wanted to meet him. I ordered a lentil soup and another water, and watched the crowds of hungry families pass me by on their way to the Mandarin.

It took longer than twenty minutes for Paolo to show up; it was more like thirty. He walked briskly up to the entrance and stood there scanning the parking lot and the inside of the restaurant through the glass. He wore black leather loafers — the kind that had tassels instead of laces. His pleated grey slacks hung at the appropriate length over the shoes, and his black golf shirt was tucked into his pants. From my vantage point I couldn't see a little Polo emblem, but I bet it was there. He wore no hat, allowing me to see that it was him from any part of the parking lot. His hair was a little bit thinner and a bit more grey. The only real difference was his posture; his shoulders were up as though tension had wound them tight. As he turned to scan the crowds of people entering and waiting inside, his whole body moved rather than just his head. Something was wrong with the old man. Something was pulling every muscle and tendon tight from the inside out.

I powered up the phone as I finished my last mouthful of soup. I ordered a plate of gyros for Paolo, sending Yousif out of the dining room to the kitchen. The phone chirped its ring in my ear, and I watched Paolo grope at his pockets through the shaded window.

"Yeah?" he said.

"Walk down along the side of the Mandarin. Turn the corner and open the gate. Inside there's a dumpster. Walk in and close the door behind you."

"You want me to meet you in a dumpster?"

"Not in, Paolo, beside. Leave the phone on while you walk."

"You're pushing it, *figlio*. I have my limits, and you are on the edge."

"Keep walking," I said as I watched Paolo walk away from the restaurant. I listened to him grumble on the phone as his body disappeared. Soon I heard the creak of a wooden door behind Paolo's complaining. I waited.

"You motherfucker. Where are you, you shit? You think this is funny? You —"

"Shut up and stand there. I'm watching you right now. I want to know who else is too."

"I came alone. Don't you get it? I'm alone. I just want to talk to you."

"Johnny didn't just want to talk," I said between sips from the glass of water on the table. That gave Paolo pause. "I told that kid exactly what I wanted him to do. I had no idea he would be so . . . overzealous."

"You send shit help and look where it gets you."

"I told you —"

"Shut up and wait there. If someone like Johnny couldn't follow your instructions there are probably others who won't too."

"That is the last time you talk to me with that disrespect. I will walk out of here and make it so you beg to see me. I'll carve an invitation into the ass of that bartender's wife. You got that? Now where the fuck are you?"

I had pushed it with Paolo, and it had shown me nothing. He didn't give up any more information. All I did was piss him off. "Give me a minute. Once I'm sure you're clean I'll pick you up."

"Once you know I'm clean?"

"It's dumpster humour, Paolo."

"You motherfucker —"

I put the phone down and watched the lot while Paolo swore. He had been out of sight for two minutes, and no one had followed after him. No one would give him that much rope if they were tailing him. They would want to know what Paolo Donati was doing beside a dumpster.

I picked the phone up again. Paolo was no longer yelling. I could only hear his heavy seething breaths. "Walk back out front and go into the Mediterranean restaurant on your right."

"You said you were picking me up. I'm not jumping through any more hoops. If you're not there, I will find a place I know you'll run to."

I didn't answer him because through the window I saw him walk back into view still yelling into his phone. I closed Johnny's phone and watched Paolo's eyes open wider in disbelief. He stopped walking and stared at the phone then at the restaurant. I waved to him from behind the glass. He glowered at me — the type of glare that had gotten other people killed. Paolo marched through the doors and sat down in front of me with his back to the glass.

"You got some nerve making me stand next to —" He was interrupted by a plate of gyros being placed in front of him. "What the fuck is this?" he asked in a tone that seemed to force a tremor through Yousif's body.

"G-g-gyros sir. Your dining companion ordered them for you, sir."

"It's cool, Yousif. He just gets grumpy when he's hungry. Don't ya, Dad?"

Paolo grumbled a response and forced a smile at our waiter. Yousif winked at me, his optimism returned. "You won't be hungry for long, sir. Enjoy."

We both watched him walk to the kitchen. It was the brisk walk of a busy man. I turned back to Paolo, who was busy himself staring at his plate.

"Try it, it's good."

Paolo sniffed the steamy food and pushed the plate away. He stared at me, and I stared back. Neither of our eyes moved, but under the table my right hand tightened

MIKE KNOWLES

around Johnny's gun in my waistband. Paolo spoke before I decided to shoot him.

"You look like shit. You know that? You smell too."

I felt my face; my beard was long and my hair was scraggly. When I pulled my hand away I saw the dirt caked under the fingernails of my tanned hand. I didn't look like I belonged in the city, but just a day ago I had fit right in on the island. I didn't say a word — I just stared into Paolo's dark, mirthless eyes.

"You know why you never went anywhere with me?"

"I'm not a people person."

"You're not family, Wilson. Family is what's important. What we do is with family, for family. You, you were good, better than most, but you weren't family, so where could it lead?"

"Did it ever occur to you that it led me where I wanted it too? It lead me to a paycheque."

"Bullshit, *figlio*. You like to fancy yourself the invisible man, and it's true you were hard to find, but you always turned up. You worked for me because you needed something, something concrete. You needed a family and we . . . we wouldn't let you in. So what did you do? You sold us out for a bartender."

I hated sitting across from a man who was trying to read me as though I were an animal on display. "That was always your problem, Paolo. You thought you were so fucking high and mighty that everyone wanted in with you. But you're half right, I did work for you because you were exactly what I needed. You and your organization had plenty of money, work, and paranoia. I worked for you for so long *because* I could never get close. Your whole set-up was perfect because I was an outsider to everyone and everything. I survived longer than most of your men and I made a hell of a lot more money because

I played it my way, not yours or your family's. I never sold you out for the bartender because there was nothing to sell. I was never with you."

Paolo laughed at me then looked away. "Maybe I'm wrong, *figlio*. Maybe I can't see people like I thought, but that doesn't change what's important."

"And that's family," I said.

"Yeah," he said, still looking away. "Family."

"What do you want, Paolo?"

He sighed and then he told me.

CHAPTER EIGHT

"My nephews are missing."

"Which ones?" I asked.

"Armando and Nicola."

"Army and Nicky?" I said. The tone made it sound like I wasn't surprised.

"What?" Paolo asked. I said nothing, so he yelled louder. "What?"

I sighed. "Those two are idiots, Paolo. You know that. Everyone tries to cover up what they do so it doesn't get back to you, but you know about them. They walk around town like big-time gangsters throwing your name and your weight around. I bet they're real scary at that private school they go to."

"You don't think I know what they do? You think I don't fucking know?" His last words ended with his fist pounding the table. "I know what they are like out there, but they are family, and now they're gone."

"What happened?" I asked.

"Week ago, their mother called me and said they didn't

come home to the house. I said they probably were out with some girls, but they still didn't come back the next day. Their phones were off, their friends hadn't seen them. They were gone. The day after that, we found out Armando's car got towed. No one was in it."

"Where was it?"

"Outside a club in Burlington," he said.

Burlington was a city outside Hamilton. The people were richer and the air was cleaner. "You call the cops?"

"The cops got half the resources I got, and no one who knows the boys will talk to the law. The boys are gone."

"So why call me? I don't even know them."

Paolo looked me in the eye. "Someone took my nephews. Someone made them disappear. Someone . . ."

As he trailed off, I understood. "You think one of your guys did it," I said.

He looked away and nodded.

"Why would anyone who worked for you make a move on the boys? It doesn't hurt you or your power base."

Paolo looked back at me and then at the table. "Lately Armando and Nicola have been using the computer. They put themselves on the Internet on this YouTube. They said some things and some names, and it all got put on the Internet."

I whistled low and found Paolo's eyes. Naming names could get you killed, even if you were the boss's nephews.

"Do you not like your food, sir?" Yousif was back.

"Not now," I said.

"Sir, we have many other dishes I can —"

I cut him off. "Not now, Yousif."

He looked at me, his optimism cracked again. He spasmed, straightened, and then made a slow walk back to the kitchen.

Paolo was still looking at me. "It sounds like they dug

their own graves," I said. "If they put names next to events."

"I know," he said quietly. "But they were family." His words hung in the air between us. They could have ignited the cold plate of food in front of him with their anger.

"You want me to find out who did it?"

"I want to know."

"You know what Army and Nicky did. They crossed a line. You can't start accusing your own people over two rats even if they have your DNA. If you knew who it was, no one would question your revenge, but to blindly go after everyone? No one will support that. And if I go around looking into it, everyone is going to know who put me up to it. This is going to dangle me in front of the city and hang you out to dry."

"I want to know." His voice was loud. Yousif dropped a plate in back, probably terrified of the outburst.

I stared into Paolo's fiery eyes. What he wanted would get me killed, and once people figured out Paolo was using me to look into his own people, he would be finished too. Paolo said family was the most important thing, but if he did this, he would betray his second family. Nothing could save him after that. Every ambitious gangster would pull a piece away from him until there was nothing left.

We shared the silence until Paolo could take no more. "I want you to find out who did this, and then I want you to give them to me."

"No," I said. "It's not a smart play."

Before I could say any more Paolo was talking. "I'm not asking, I'm telling you. You're going to do it, or I'm going to finish things with the bartender. You and him killed Tommy and his family for what? His slut wife? If you're not in with me, *figlio*, then I'll do it alone, but before I go down, I'll make things right with the bartender by first making things right with his missus. Once I use her up, I'll put that

Irish dog down in the street. Then I'll find the fuck responsible for my nephews myself."

My hand pulsated on the gun under the table. I thought about killing Paolo in the restaurant, killing him and leaving, but he would have insurance.

As if reading my thoughts, he spoke. "I got people watching them now. I can do it from beyond the grave if I have to."

Paolo had me and he knew it. My only connection to the city could still hurt me no matter how far I ran. I rubbed my jaw, forcing the muscles to relax and my teeth to stop grinding. "Who did Army and Nicky name?" I asked.

"Bombedieri, Perino, and Rosa."

"What did they say?"

"You can see for yourself," he said, and reached into his pants.

I tensed and he said, "Easy, *figlio.*"

He produced a piece of paper folded over twice. He left it beside the cold plate and stood up. "Call me when you have a name. And I don't want none of this to lead back to me. I go down, I'm taking mister and missus Irish with me, and those two have a lot farther to fall than I do."

He waved goodbye to Yousif, who moved out from the kitchen to hold the door for him. "Nice place you got here," Paolo said.

"Thank you, sir," Yousif said timidly.

"You should think about serving some pasta, not this foreign shit. Even the Chinese place over there has pasta; it's covered in their shit sauces, but it's pasta. That's probably why they're so busy all the time."

"Thank you, sir. Have a good night." It was as rude as Yousif could let himself be.

Paolo left with a smile. I watched him go, noticing his shoulders were a bit less tense.

CHAPTER NINE

I unfolded the paper Paolo had left me. Handwritten in thick black script were three lists under three headings: Bombedieri, Perino, and Rosa. Each list had addresses, names, and descriptions like "#2" written beside the names. I assumed the addresses Paolo gave me were work and not home. I checked the paper over twice, front and back, finding only one address for each name. Paolo certainly had access to that kind of information, but having someone dig it up would surely lead to questions later. At the bottom of the paper was a website URL for a specific page on YouTube. This must have been where all of the trouble started.

The Internet was not something I had used often, but as the world changed around me and threatened to leave me behind, I versed myself in its basic functions. I knew there were people who could swim through the electrical currents of the World Wide Web like a shark, seizing any information that was appropriately juicy. The rapidly advancing technological age created more and more people like that every day, and that would make it harder for me to remain anonymous forever; it would be impossible if, like Army and Nicky, I posted my face and opinions online. The Internet was like a gun. Any random thoughts or comments shot out from a computer keyboard in the form of a binary bullet could not be retrieved. It existed in some form in the ether, and there was no chance of erasing its existence or denying it had happened. I wondered about the bullet Army and Nicky fired on YouTube, and what kind of damage it had caused.

I folded the paper up and put it into my pocket. I paid the tab and waited patiently for Yousif to come out and hold the door for me. As he approached, I saw that his jaw was set. My guest had been rude to him a few minutes ago, and he was finding it hard to remain a good host.

"Goodbye, sir," he said in a polite, curt way.

"Good luck with the dinner rush tonight, Yousif."

All at once, his pleasant demeanour broke through. "It will be very busy, sir. Very busy indeed."

The door swung awkwardly closed behind me as Yousif had another tremor. His arm tightened on the door, and it stopped moving before it formed a seal. I heard him sigh with relief as the spell ended. As I entered the parking lot, I could hear him continue talking to himself. "Very busy soon. No rest tonight."

He was right, I wouldn't rest tonight — not ever, I feared.

It had been almost two years since I had been in the city. It was possible that the last few Internet cafés I had used were still in business, but it was more likely that they were gone. Most small businesses in the downtown core quickly went the way of the dodo. None of them survived long in the infertile concrete. The city reached out and drained the businesses dry with stagnation, or it started to work on the employees, killing their bodies with pollution or their minds with constant vandalism and robbery. The old places didn't matter. I didn't want to set foot in the downtown core before I had to. Every street corner had eyes, eyes looking to pass on information for a score.

I pulled the car onto Upper James and drove north, admiring the economic prosperity the Hamilton mountain enjoyed. Everything was different a few hundred metres in the air. The cars were sleeker and quieter, and the stores were bright and busy. As I drove closer and closer to the core, the stores got smaller and smaller, as though they were tightening in preparation for the city's assault.

Eventually, as I neared the escarpment access, I found a used computer store that had spawned from a decades old two-storey house. I parked the car on a side street and made my way around front to the door. The original front door had been replaced by a glass door encased in a heavy mesh with thick reinforced bars. The door had "Cam's Computer Den" stencilled at eye level. I pushed it open and immediately felt the heat of multiple computer hard drives and the warm bodies of several cats. The warm stale air rushed at the door like a genie escaping from a bottle.

A voice came out from behind a counter piled up with old computer keyboards and monitors. "Hep you?"

"What?" I said as I approached the counter.

"Ken I hep you?"

I saw a man hunched over a desk; he wore a headband that held a magnifying lens in front of his face. The desk light in front of him beamed an impossibly bright light down on the soldering iron in his right hand. He was a heavy man in the way that refrigerators were heavy. The back of his neck had a roll of fat that bulged out as though it were going to burst. His plaid shirt was a vast tight expanse over his back, stretching the pattern into something that resembled a magic eye poster. He sat on a stool with his legs spread wide apart. I imagined his almost-splits was only possible because it was necessary — he had to have a place for his stomach to rest while he was off his feet. His garbled speech was because of a piece of metal he was holding between his pursed lips.

"I need to use the Internet," I said.

The man barely turned. "Don't do dat here, I dust fix compuders."

"You have to have Internet access here. I just need it for a few minutes."

"Go find an Internet café."

"Twenty bucks for five minutes."

He turned all the way around so I could see his face. His goatee pushed itself out of the heavy fat folds in his face. One of his eyes was huge in the magnifying lens. He pulled the piece of metal out of his mouth with a fat hand, its skin straining like a full water balloon.

"You think I'm fucking stupid?"

I stared at him, unmoved by his question.

"I'm not leaving you alone with my equipment so I can be on the hook for whatever shit you wanna download."

"Listen —"

"No, you listen. Take your money and go look at your sick shit somewhere else."

I had had enough of the fat man. It may have been sitting with Paolo and taking his threats, or the stunt Johnny pulled on the island. Whatever it was, I was tired of assholes. I walked around the counter towards the fat man and his headband. As I got closer, his magnified eye twitched faster and faster. Finally, he put his hand up to his face and lifted the monacle. His fat hand obscured his vision for a second, hiding my rising palm. I gripped his nose and squeezed. Immediately his eyes watered and his huge paws enveloped mine. The fact that he worked with his hands all day made his grip on my hand like a bear trap. I didn't mind losing my hold on his nose; I let go so I could get my left hand on his Adam's apple.

My fingers dug deep into his fleshy neck, finding the small cartilage box in his throat. His voice involuntarily squeaked, and his huge hands rushed to mine again. His grip was powerful, but mine was better, and this time I had no interest in letting go. All the time spent on the fishing boat made my grip like a pit bull's jaws. The fat man's hands slid came away empty as he pawed at his neck. His hands continued to work at my fist, but they slackened when I applied pressure. The fragile cartilage in his neck bent under the strain, and his throat closed, sending the fat man to his knees. The immense pain was nothing compared to the lack of oxygen. His enormous body required a vast amount of air to stay vertical; I imagined it was supplied in huge gasping breaths twenty-four hours a day. Cutting off the air was a viscous shock to his already weak system.

As his face reddened, I leaned in close. "I'm no pervert, I just need to use the Internet for five minutes. You can stay in the room with me if you don't believe me."

I let go of his throat and listened to his breathing start again. It sounded like a steam engine starting to move. "Forty," he said between gasps.

"What?"

"Forty for the Internet. You said twenty. I want forty. Forty gets you the Internet, and I won't call the cops about the choking thing."

"I could just finish the job and shove a buffalo wing down your throat. The cops would buy that."

"Then you wouldn't have the password for the Internet. You'd have to go somewhere else. Be a pain in the ass killing me and then having to drive around town to find an Internet connection and a buffalo wing to bring back here. All that work for forty bucks." He seemed to smile under his hands, which were rubbing his nose and throat simultaneously.

I pulled out two twenties and put them on the counter. "Show me the computer."

CHAPTER TEN

The fat man told me his name was Louis while he pulled off the headband and unplugged the soldering iron. He said he'd always been into computers and after his parents died he just moved up from the basement into the rest of the house. The shop sprung out of the constant piles of circuitry he accumulated around the house. He locked the front door and flipped off the open sign then led me into the back room to a desktop computer.

Louis brought the computer out of sleep mode with a fat finger. He opened an icon and entered a password I noted to be a random sequence of letters and numbers. He was right, if I had choked him out, the computer would have been useless. Once Internet Explorer was working, Louis took a step back and opened his hands in a gesture that said, "It's all yours."

I stood in front of the computer and called up the site Paolo had scribbled on the piece of paper he gave me. A black box appeared on the screen with a play button in the centre. I clicked the button and watched the file load, and do something it called buffering, in a matter of seconds. Beside the loading screen, I saw thumbnails of other posts by the boys — there were at least fifteen. Fifteen times at least, Army and Nicky had put themselves out on the Internet and let their mouths run.

"Fast connection," I said.

"Oh yeah. Once you go high speed, there's no going back. I can download a song in thirty seconds —" The computer interrupted him as it began to play the file. "Who are they?"

Two teenagers appeared on the screen in the little play window. Army and Nicky were brothers who were only a year apart, but they could have passed as twins. Both boys had tall over-gelled hair that stood in shiny triangular peaks. Their white teeth gleamed in their almost identical acne-speckled faces. Both boys got their father's pointy nose and their mother's full lips. The boys were pretty, not handsome.

All of their prettiness ended when their mouths opened. They spoke in loud profane street language that all at once sounded inauthentic. It sounded as though they were mimicking the way they thought a real hip-hop gangster might speak.

"Holla at your boyz! The Donati crew is back on the air," Army said. "We still be bringing the thug to the world and ain't nobody going to stop us, ya heard."

"Nobody gonna stand in the way a tha' Donati crew, we gotz mad guerrilla tactics, yo." Nicky brandished a gun, which came into view when he added his two cents.

Army went on, "We got the roots everywhere — in the Hammer, even in the U fucking S. We the princes of the city. All of it gonna be ours. It's ours by blood. We own this rock."

"I'm gonna get me a blinged-out crown," Nicky chimed in while mimicking putting a crown on his head.

"Those goombahs won't be able to hold on ta what is rightfully ours. Fuckin' Bombedieri thinks he's big shit running numbers. Oh the 'Bomb' is the man all right . . . with his calculator. Dom the Bomb is a real Texas Instrument kind of gangster. He's got a long way to go before he gets respect." Army made a gun with his index finger and thumb and shot the camera when he mentioned respect.

Nicky spoke up again, building on Army's revelation about Bombedieri. "Shit, Perino thinks he's big time 'cause he pimps shit out of that store of his."

Both boys stopped and did a silent sign of the cross, their faces suddenly angelic, before they started laughing.

Nicky continued, "He hasn't pulled a trigger on a gat since he killed Carerra four years ago. He thinks he's gold 'cause he shot that fucker into his soup. But gold gets tarnished, yo."

"Bitch," Army yelled.

"Bi-atch," Nicky confirmed.

"Rosa is tough," Army said. "I hear that boy pulled the trigger nine times last year."

"I hear that boy pulled a lot of triggers last year . . . with his teeth." Nicky delivered the joke with all the glee of a child telling his first knock-knock joke, and then both boys laughed at their apparent outing of Rosa while making dick-sucking gestures with their hands and cheeks.

"It's our time," Army said. "It's time the Donati crew showed the Hammer how real thugs do."

Nicky pulled off his shirt to expose a tattoo across his chest. It read "gangster" in big black Gothic letters. "We ain't into playing, we into being. 'Cause that's how we roll."

Both boys high-fived. "It's our time," Army said again and then he reached forward off the screen. Suddenly, booming rap music pounded out of the computer speakers.

The music was too distorted with bass to be understandable. After a minute of music and on-screen posturing by the boys, the screen went black. The site offered the option to view the other postings by the boys. I scrolled down the screen instead of opening more of the videos. There were comments from viewers all the way down the screen. Most thought the boys were a joke; many were scathing in their hatred of Army and Nicky.

"What a bunch of douche bags," Louis said. I nodded in silent agreement. "I mean . . . they're white kids. They look like such posers. No one could take that crap seriously."

This time I didn't nod. Louis was wrong; someone took these boys real serious. These two morons crossed a line. Crossed it so far that even genetics couldn't save them. They didn't just slip up and say the wrong thing at the wrong time; they broadcast names, crimes, and gossip for the world to hear. And here I was having to put it all on the line to find these two jokes.

"Why did you pay forty bucks for this?" Louis asked.

"I had to see it before I started," I said as I clicked the tools folder and erased the browser history.

"Started what?"

I didn't answer Louis's question, I just got up and walked to the door.

"Do you know those kids?" Louis asked.

I didn't answer as I opened the door. I didn't know those kids, and after seeing the video I was pretty sure no one who did would ever be able to recognize them again.

n the car, I sat with the air conditioning on while I fiddled with the radio and used my thumb to loosen the muscles in my jaw. The rough massage gave me a break from the constant grinding of teeth I had since I met with Paolo. I passed stations pumping out unfamiliar music by even more unfamiliar groups. Music had become even more artificial since I dropped off the radar. I spent too much time on the boat listening to the rhythmic beat of a fish finder, out of range of anything that could transmit the changing popular culture. I turned off the radio, realizing it was keeping me in place when I should have been moving.

I pulled the car back into traffic and drove the Hamilton mountain. I found Stonechurch Road, which ran the length of the city, and settled into its stop-and-go rhythm. While I sat at a light, I powered up Johnny's phone and called Paolo. He picked up without saying a word.

"Can you talk?" I asked.

"Not now."

"I'll call back in ten minutes," I said. I heard an animal

grunt before the line disconnected. Paolo was angry that I gave him an order. He was even angrier that he couldn't do a thing about it. Once Paolo was off the line, I dialled another number from memory; it was a number I knew would still work.

"Sully's Tavern," Steve's voice said after two rings.

"Do you ever take the night off?" I asked.

The reply came immediately. "Some of us can't pick up and leave at a moment's notice."

"How you doing, Steve?"

"Good." His surprise was over, and he was back to his usual short responses. "You in town?"

"Yeah."

"I have your money and those tools you told me about. I took it all after Sandra and I cleaned the place up."

"You took Sandra to clean up the office?" I asked.

"I told her where I was going, and she said she wanted to come."

I marvelled at Steve and his relationship with Sandra. I spent every waking moment trying to stay off the grid, trying to keep every interaction transient, and here was my only friend, a person connected at the hip to his wife. He told her everything and didn't even think about a need for secrets. For a quiet second on the phone, alone in my car, I envied his attachment like a paraplegic envied a sprinter.

"Any problems?"

"Nah, wife thinks you need help decorating though. You working?"

"That's why I called."

"Where?" Steve was ready to meet me, to do whatever. In his mind he could never repay the debt he thought he owed me.

"It's not like that. I got found, and someone we know pulled me back here for a job."

"How did you get pulled?" It sounded as though Steve was suddenly speaking through clenched teeth. Steve knew what I was like; he knew there was very little that could force me to do anything. He knew he and Sandra were about the only leverage someone could use on me. He was starting to see red, and I had to derail him before he put down the phone. Steve had the capabilities of a dirty bomb. He could absolutely destroy everything around him, but worse than that, the carnage left from his explosion would be felt for years to come.

"Steve," I said to no response. "Steve . . . Christ, Steve, listen to me. I'll tell you how I got pulled back, but you have to hear me out. Are you listening? You can take care of this but you have to hear me out."

"Tell me."

Steve's quick response fazed me for a second. He was listening more than I thought. Maybe things had changed since I had been gone.

"I thought you would have been out in the street by now."

"Things change," he said, reading my mind.

"So you'll cool it and let things play out my way?"

"Things haven't changed that much. Tell me."

"A guy came to see me; he told me to come home. After a long talk, I found out why."

"Tell me straight — no one is listening."

"You don't know that," I said, thinking of Paolo.

"I do, Wilson. Now tell me straight."

I figured I owed Steve the truth. "Paolo found me," I said.

"You were fishing on film."

I pulled over to a chorus of honking horns and punched the dashboard. "That fucking picture," I said.

"Ben saw it. He loves fishing and he showed me the fish

when he saw it on the front page. Big guy didn't even know who the politician was. I saw the fish and I saw you. The beard looks good."

Ben was a giant of a man who grew up on a farm in rural Ontario. He still clung to his roots, often wearing overalls to tend bar. Steve hired him after Sandra was kidnapped. Ben's job was to keep her safe when Steve stepped out. Ben was capable; I had seen him break up brawls alone. The brawlers weren't punks either — they were hard men. Ben blasted through them with giant fists like Thor with two flesh-and-bone hammers.

"Paolo saw the picture and sent a guy out to see me."

"He dead?" Steve asked.

I didn't answer the question. "I got in touch with Paolo, and he told me he needed me for a job."

"Doing what?"

"Job doesn't matter. What's important is he said he had a man watching you."

"Yeah?" Steve's answers were getting shorter. Soon it would be grunts then blood.

"Whoever it is, he's watching you to make sure I play ball."

"When?"

"Over the next day or two."

"No. When can I deal with this?"

I smiled. "You have changed. Two years ago you would have your hair up, and you'd have been in the street already."

"I am in the street — phone's portable."

"Don't do anything yet. I can fix it."

"When?"

"Give me a day, two max. Find whoever's watching and keep tabs on him. Wait for my call before you do anything. I can fix this, and then he'll be gone and everything will be cool."

"I think I already found him," Steve said.

I pressed the phone harder into my ear out of fear that Steve could instantly make the situation infinitely worse. "Will you wait for my call?"

I heard traffic digitized through the phone lines. Then Steve sighed and answered. "Two days. Any more, and I can't promise anything."

"This guy can't get beaten to death on the street; that will just bring more heat. If he goes, it's got to be quiet, like he didn't exist. Once I handle my end, no one can know what your stalker was up to. That means no one can find him."

"Call me when I can move."

I said goodbye and hung up the phone. I nosed the car into traffic again, hearing fewer horns than when I pulled over, and moved back towards Upper James and the Mediterranean restaurant I was at an hour before. Traffic had come to life since I had been online. The roads were clogged like the tunnels in an ant farm. It was like the mountain was channelling downtown just for me. I looked around at the frustrated commuters and smiled. I enjoyed the feeling of being back in the city. With each breath, I felt like I was uploading what I was, one file at a time. I felt more like myself than I had in a long time. The only problem was the scraggly reflection in the rearview. I didn't look like me — which wasn't a bad thing — but I didn't look like anyone else from around here either — which certainly was. I would stand out in a crowd to almost anyone, and I wasn't about to go up against just anyone; I was going to tamper with the lives of dangerous men. Dangerous men who would notice an unkempt loner in their periphery.

At the third red light, I rolled down the window so I could smell the black diesel leaving the bus in front of me. I lost myself in the smell of the city in some sort of grey-concrete zen daze. The fumes mingled with the roar of the bus engine, dulling the cell phone chirp from the seat beside me. I got my head in the window and opened the phone on its third ring.

"You want me to call you back, stay off the line," Paolo said.

"I saw the video," I said.

"Something, ain't it? Stupid kids are like parrots repeating everything they hear." Paolo never stopped comparing people to animals. He loved to show everyone how low they were on the food chain compared to him.

"Parrots are smart, though, aren't they?"

"Being capable of speech doesn't make anything smart. Let's see a parrot make me an omelette. That would be one smart fucking bird."

Traffic picked up and I stayed right, riding the slow lane back to the plaza. "The video, they mention three names," I said.

"*Figlio,* I gave you all the information you need. Did those two years make you soft? You never needed me to hold your hand before."

"I never had to wipe your nose before," I said, and instinctively moved the phone away from my ear to avoid what was to come.

"You little fuck!" Paolo screamed. "You think because I asked you for help you're worth all this trouble? I let you go as long as I did because you were on the back burner. You never got out, you never left; I just put you on pause. If you want, I can finish this myself, but if I do then I don't need you. And if I don't need you, what the fuck do I need the bartender for? Not to mention those nice people who own the boat you were working on."

I knew the threats would come and I still walked into it. I cursed myself for being so hotheaded. Deep down, though, I wasn't mad at Paolo, or my temper. I was scared that I wasn't what I had been anymore after being away for so long. If I couldn't do what needed to be done, it wouldn't be Paolo who killed my friends, it would be me.

I could still hear Paolo seething on the phone. I decided to ignore the outburst. "I never needed you to hold my hand before because I knew all of the players on the board. I don't know these names that well."

"You only fuck over people you know? That why you screwed me over for the bartender?" Paolo was still acting petulant after two years.

"Who are they to you? Are they important?"

"After you whacked the Commie bees' nest, they swarmed all over us. They knew our people and our business. They had been planning to take us out for a long time, and someone had fed them current information. A lot of people died or just disappeared. Those Russian fucks tried to take all the leaders away so the family would just fall apart. I had to promote prematurely to fix all of the holes. Bombedieri, Perino, and Rosa got an early leg up, but they were eager and they were workers. We hit that bees' nest back hard. Bees calm down around smoke, so we lit a whole lot of fucking fires."

"How important are they to you?"

"They're family, but they're not *family*. They got to move up pretty high pretty quick and so they never spent the years making connections or learning how to act. They're a rough crew — not at all like their predecessors, but they earn in spades. They're big players, but they got no real support. They could be gone tomorrow and no one would cry about it. They made enemies out of a lot of the people they left behind when they became management. People who were none too cheery about their sudden advancement. No one comes right out and says it, but I heard whispers."

"From Army and Nicky?" I interrupted.

"I never talked business with them because they were never going to take over."

"Anyone tell them that?"

Paolo was silent for a moment, then he spoke quietly. "They were never in this life. They went to private school, for Christ's sake."

"So did you."

"These kids ain't me. They don't have the instinct. Even back then, in those schools, I had it — everyone knew. My nephews never even showed interest in this life. They liked the money and the respect, but any sign of trouble and they'd cry to their mother. I never told them no 'cause everyone knew they were never going to go to work."

"Everyone but them," I said, more to myself than to Paolo. "You saw that tattoo, heard that music. They thought they were in the life already. They acted like they had a crew and they were the up-and-comers."

"Stupid parrots," he said.

"What I want to know is, who is the most likely to move on your family?"

"None of them. They're made. They know the rules."

Rules. There was a time when I tried to speak to Paolo about rules. "You told me there were no rules, only the law of the jungle."

"There are rules if I say so."

"Fine," I said. "Who's got the most balls, and the most pride?"

Paolo thought about it for a second. "Bombedieri," he said.

"Army and Nicky said he was just a numbers guy."

"And I told you they were never involved in the day-to-day business. That shit they said on the Internet was garbage. You don't get to *just* be a numbers guy — we aren't the Ontario gaming commission. Dom Bombedieri spent a lot of time getting everyone in the neighbourhood on side with how he runs things. Everybody: the police, the Russians, even those Chink gangs stay clear of his rackets. But there was a time they didn't, and he made sure everyone knew where he stood about that by making a lot of people lay down, *capisce?* That's how he got the name 'Dom the Bomb.' My nephews would have had no idea about what he was into, or what he did to get into it."

"So he's not the pushover Army and Nicky said he was."

Paolo laughed. "I don't promote pushovers. Bombedieri's as bad as they come — more so now that he works quiet. He's like a pike. You ever see one of those? Ugly fish — all scale and bone. But it comes up under bugs on the surface and takes them without warning. That's what Dom the Bomb is like now that he's in charge. No one sees him coming."

I wondered if Army and Nicky saw him coming when they disappeared. If it was him at all. "The address you gave me for him. What is it?"

"His uncle Guy runs a cleaning-supply store. Dom uses part of it as his office. He's got his own entrance out back and he and his crew run their business out of it. He is in charge of everything west of James Street."

"Big chunk," I interrupted.

"I told you, I don't promote pushovers. He took over that part of town when Lolli and Porco disappeared. It was a lot of territory to take over, especially with those Ivans hitting made men, but Dom made it work. He runs that part of town for me, and he does it real well now that he's learned a thing or two."

"Who's his number two?"

"*Figlio*, I gave you a list. The list had all the information you need. I didn't bring you home so we could play phone tag like a couple a fruits. Use the list and get the fucking job done."

"One last thing. Tell me about his number two."

Paolo sighed. "It's a kid named Denis. Denis is Dom's cousin on his father's side. All I know is Dom vouches for him. I don't micromanage everyone's operations. As long as the money comes in, I don't give a shit who's on staff. Dom vouches for him, and that is enough because if something gets fucked it's Dom who will be responsible."

"He at the store a lot?"

Paolo began to get annoyed. "Yeah, a lot. His father owns it. He's always there. He makes sure his old man never has to get involved with Dom's business."

"How old —"

"No more questions *figlio*, not a one. You get out to these men and you start finding things out. Don't call me again unless you have good news for me. I'm not playing twenty questions while you waste my time. Got it? If I have to I'll give you some incentive to work harder, but I don't think the bartender would like that."

"I just don't want to be in the dark again. You did that to me before."

Paolo's voice became low and he spoke slowly enunciating each word carefully so that there was no way I would misconstrue the threat. "I am almost sorry I brought you into this at all. When I am totally sorry, I will make sure that you feel worse."

I hung up the phone without saying goodbye. I didn't worry about Paolo's threats. He never threatened me before; he never had to. With Paolo, you always had one bite at the apple before he forced it down your throat. The constant threats meant Paolo was in a bad situation. I had to make sure I knew everything I could, so I didn't go down with Paolo like some kind of kamikaze.

I parked the car back in the restaurant parking lot and looked around at the other stores in the plaza while waiting for Paolo to show. I saw the Mandarin looming huge from the concrete taking up five storefronts. Beside it was a shoe store, then a chain discount-clothing store, a religious paraphernalia shop, and a menswear chain. Mark's Work Wearhouse sold clothing for construction workers and professionals alike. I got out of the car and walked straight through the crowded lot full of hungry buffet seekers to the automatic doors of Mark's Work Wearhouse. I breezed through the entrance past the registers to the menswear section.

I found several different types of pants hanging on display racks. I passed the denim and lighter-colour pants until I stopped in front of a dark brown pair of cotton pants. The material was durable and advertised as wrinkle-resistant. I flipped through the rack and pulled my size to hold them up in the light so I could examine the pants front and back.

"They got secret pockets too," a woman's voice said. An older woman with short blond hair and an athletic build approached me from behind a rack of clothes. "Sewn into the leg are concealed pockets. You can carry all kinds of things in the pants and no one would ever know. My husband carries his BlackBerry and one of them multi-tools; you know the kind, with the pliers and all those gadgets. People are always so surprised when he gets them out because you honestly can't tell where he gets them from."

"Perfect," I said. "I need a T-shirt to go with the pants and something heavier to wear if it gets cold."

"No problem," the saleswoman said. She walked two aisles over and pulled out a black T-shirt with a little pocket on the front. "You look like a large."

While I felt the shirt's cotton material, the woman found a black lightweight jacket made of a water resistant material. "You can wear this zipped or unzipped depending on how cold it gets."

"They're both great," I said. "All I need is boots."

She looked down at my old boots, stained by fish and boat grease. "You sure do. Those need to go wherever it is boots go to die. You want something similar?"

I stared at my boots, realizing that I hadn't noticed how gross they were. I looked up and nodded.

"I know how it is when you love a pair of shoes, believe me. I still have shoes I wore in high school. Can you believe that? High school. They're too small now. Funny how shoes get smaller. But I could never part with them — sentimental reasons, you know. I'll find you a nice pair of boots so you won't feel too great a loss. Follow me."

Not more than a minute later, I had a dark pair of steel-toed boots that looked a lot like the boots on my feet must have once. I took all my things to the register and paid cash for everything. As I shovelled the change into my pocket, I asked where the nearest drugstore was. The teenage cashier told me that there was one of the chain drugstores on the other side of the plaza.

I stowed my new clothes in the trunk of the car and walked around the plaza past a video store and used-record shop to the Shoppers Drug Mart. The store was located in an adjacent plaza that had spawned off the one I was in like a tumour. The plaza had a retail chain drugstore, supermarket, and pet store, as well as an unemployment office, and a gym. No one who used the unemployment office could afford the goods offered by the big-box stores in the plaza. The prices were only deals to the middle class. Everyone else had to trudge farther into the city to find deals on items that the bigger chain stores had already rejected.

MIKE KNOWLES

The Shoppers Drug Mart had the same smell in every store. The perfumes and colognes mingled with the antiseptic smell of the pharmacy to create a scent that could be found nowhere in nature. The chain store had almost anything anyone could ever want. Eventually, I thought, every store could be a Shoppers Drug Mart.

I immediately found the men's aisle and picked up a razor and an electric hair clipper. As I searched for the rest of the toiletries I would need, I found the stationery aisle. At the end of the row beside the different notepads was a digital recorder. It had a back-to-school sale sticker on it, and I figured it was something university students would use to record their professors. The item was in a locked display case, and it took me five minutes to flag down an employee to get it out. Ten minutes after that, I was back at the car loading more bags into the trunk.

I wasn't hungry so soon after eating with Paolo, but I would be in a few hours. I decided to stock up on some food to eat later. I had already exposed myself several times buying clothes and toiletries in busy stores. I hated being in the open around so many people, but it was something that had to be done. I knew that I would be unrecognizable to most of the people I encountered once I shed my clothes and beard, but I still wasn't happy. It was a long shot that someone would recognize me at this plaza after almost two years away, but I was having no luck with long shots. I had already gotten my face in every major publication in the country, which was something I thought impossible until it happened. I had interacted with enough new faces already, so I decided to make my way back to the Mediterranean restaurant. I found Yousif waiting just inside the doors — alone.

"Hello again, sir. Are you hungry again? Well, you came just in time. Very soon we will be busy."

"I need some takeout. Something that will keep for a few hours. Can you get something together?"

"What would you like, sir?"

"You decide what's best. You're the restauranteur."

After a twitch that was part pride and part surprise, Yousif was off to the kitchen. He was so excited that he didn't say another word. Two sales in one day must have been a record.

I walked around the empty restaurant looking at each of the immaculate tables in the dining room. I mentally went over what I had bought. I had clothes, stuff to clean myself up with, and a gun. I ran my hands over my hair and was thankful I bought the clippers. My hands moved down my neck to my lower back, and I stretched, feeling the muscles loosen slightly. My hands felt the hard sheath of my fishing knife. I smiled to myself and added the knife to my checklist.

The knife and the gun would get me by, but eventually I would run through the six remaining shots in the revolver. I needed a tool to make conversations easier, something less loud and bloody. It was hard to get someone to talk after you shot them, and a knife was only as good as your resolve to use it, and once you cut someone they weren't quiet — even the hard ones screamed. I wanted a sap, but finding a sap would force me to mingle with more people. The kind of people who lived in the core of the city. Those type of people would be more in my element, and they had memories like elephants. There would be a good chance I would be recognized even with the fisherman's disguise I wore. The food came and interrupted my train of thought.

"I gave you a wonderful selection of tapas and —"

"I trust you, Yousif; it smells great. Thank you for taking the time to make this up for me. I know you are busy getting ready for the dinner rush. What do I owe you?"

MIKE KNOWLES

Yousif beamed with pride and looked around his empty restaurant, mentally going over all the chores to complete before no one showed up. "No charge, sir."

"How much, Yousif?"

"You have been good to me today. I only ask that you return with a guest for a full meal, and that the guest not be the man you brought earlier."

I laughed and said goodbye to Yousif, promising to return for a proper dinner. I was amazed at how easy it was to make a friend. I realized it happened because I put myself out there. I made myself noticeable — something I spent a lifetime trying to avoid. I swore inwardly at myself and wondered if I had lost a step. I wondered if I would survive the next few days so out of practice. My frustration was interrupted by a small dog, which found its way under my foot. The dog yelped, then growled.

"Watch where you're going," an old woman said. Her hair was puffed with extra aerosol hairspray, making it almost transparent. Her scalp showed through the hair like a glossy, veined egg. The dog made me think of different canines I had come in contact with over the years. One mean dog in particular split his time guarding a bookie and gnawing on a heavy rubber bone. I remembered the bone in particular because as a teenager I picked it up to play a game of tug with the dog. The animal stared at me, shocked, before latching on to my sleeve. I screamed and dropped the bone, trying to escape a game of tug I then wanted no part of. The bookie screamed too, and told the dog to let me go, but nothing happened. I watched helplessly as the dog's eyes met mine for a split second before disappearing in a blur. The shake of its powerful head almost pulled my arm out of the socket. The dog paused and growled, preparing for another shake. As the attack started, another movement caught my eye. The heavy chew toy hit the dog behind the ear, as he closed his eyes and wrenched at my arm. The blow was so fast nothing in the room had time to prepare a reaction. The dog fell sideways as though it were suddenly struck by lightning, and my arm came free.

"Keep your dog under control, or I'm gonna think you have no discipline. I don't work with people who got no discipline." My uncle's voice registered no shock at what had just happened. The only giveaway that he was agitated at all was the veins bulging from his forehead.

"Sure, sure, Rick. The dog just wanted to play. Got carried away is all. We can still do business. You're okay, eh, kid," the bookie said as he came around the desk and put a leash on the unconscious dog. "Come on, ya worthless fleabag, get out back." The limp dog was dragged by the leash out the back door.

While the bookie was out of sight, my uncle leaned into me. "The dog was just trying to keep what was his. Remember that. If an inbred mutt will go that far for a piece of rubber, imagine what someone will do to you for money. There's always dogs looking to take a bite."

I nodded my head and rubbed my shoulder, but I never looked up. I stared at the chew toy still on the floor, glossy with drool.

I took the food with me on a stroll around the sidewalk of the plaza. Within minutes, I was in front of the giant pet store. The store advertised huge deals to customers with one of the pet store cards, and other monumental deals to those without. I walked inside and ambled around the empty aisles past the fish tanks and birdseed until I came to the dog accessories aisle. I didn't think dog accessories warranted a whole aisle, but I was wrong. There were dozens of bones among the hundreds of toys made by just as many manufacturers.

I walked the aisle twice before stopping at a heavy rubber bone meant for big dogs like pit bulls and mastiffs. I bent the heavy bone in its cardboard packaging, noting its give. The bone would work perfect. Swinging it back would bend the rubber slightly, forcing it to snap forward, adding momentum, when it was swung in the other direction. It was a good, hard sap.

I paid for the bone and took it and the food to the car. I edged out into traffic and drove Upper James once again. It took three minutes for me to find an airport motel. It was a place in between cheap and expensive, offering rides to the nearby Hamilton International Airport and convenient entertainment at the next-door Hooters and Italian restaurant.

CHAPTER TWELVE

I paid for a room with cash, leaving a small deposit I was prepared to never see again. I brought all of my bags into the room and spread the contents on the bed. I opened the food and ate a piece of oily grilled bread while I decided what to do first.

By the time I finished the bread, I was stripped and ready to plug the clippers in. I stood over the sink in the cramped bathroom with the clippers set to the second-lowest setting. Each pass over my head sent hair into the sink in greasy clumps. The dead hair smelled of the boats and fish. The odour was deep in the hair and would never have washed out; it was as much a part of the hair as the colour.

It took ten minutes to cut my hair. Once I was sure I had gotten every spot, I set the clippers down a notch and began trimming my beard. The dark coarse hairs fell like dandelion spores into the sink. I trimmed everything down and began shaving the shortened facial hair into a presentable beard. It wouldn't stand out in the city anymore, but it would obscure a face some people might remember. With my appearance acceptable, I got in the shower.

I unwrapped the motel soap and used half the bar to get the last summer's worth of work on the boat off of me. Each swirl down the drain brought a bit more of me back. I was less the fisherman and more the invisible man with each passing minute under the water.

I quickly towelled off and, without dressing, ate the rest of Yousif's food on the bed. Beads of water dampened the comforter, but I didn't pay the dampness any mind. After my dinner, I threw everything on the bed onto the floor — except the revolver. I propped my head up on the pillows and used my left hand to control the television remote. I watched television in the dark, catching up on reruns and flicking by newer shows I had never heard of. I fell asleep alone in the dark, one hand on the remote, the other reflexively curled around the revolver.

I woke the next afternoon and put on the new clothes. The pants and shirts had fold lines in them, but I was sure they would fade away. I didn't feel bad about the twelve hours' sleep I had; the past few days wound me tight, and the next few would not be any easier.

I retrieved the belt from my old pants and put it on, making sure the knife was concealed behind my back under my shirt. I tried to put the gun into my waistband, but it was too noticeable under the knife, and too bulky under the front of my T-shirt. I had almost given up on carrying the gun on me at all when I remembered the hidden pockets in the pants. The gun fit tight into a concealed thigh pocket. It wasn't good for a quick draw, but it was much better than leaving the gun in the car.

I picked up the toiletries, clippers, old clothes, and garbage and put them all into a pillowcase. I figured the pillowcase was more than a fair trade for my deposit. I had to take everything with me. The takeout containers would lead to Yousif and then to a description of me and Paolo.

I left the room key on the dresser and made it to my car without being noticed. I drove into the next parking lot I saw and emptied the pillowcase into three separate dumpsters. I had to individually force each item under the padlocked chains holding the lids closed. Once everything was gone, I got back in the car and drove towards the mountain access. Upper James led down the mountain, becoming James Street when it left the rocky incline. The road was just as worn and craggy as I remembered and it bounced me around inside the car. I caught sight of my reflection and noticed the change in my appearance. My face was more different, and more the same, than it had been in a long while. A fact that made me smile.

I found the cleaning-supply store that Dom Bombedieri ran his crew out of and spent the next few minutes circling the neighbourhood. There were kids outside hanging out even though it was 1:30 p.m. on a school day. None of the kids was doing anything wrong; they just hung around or played keep-away with basketballs. None of the kids eyed me twice as I circled, so I wrote them off as lookouts. I pulled to the curb two storefronts away from the cleaning-supply store and opened the glovebox. I pulled out the cell phone, mini recorder, and dog bone, then shifted in my seat to load the phone and recorder into a pants pocket concealed near my calf. After that, I reached into the back seat and picked up the jacket.

I got out of the car and put the coat on, leaving it unzipped. The bone fit into a pocket on the side of the jacket, leaving five or six inches hanging out. I didn't care because it didn't appear threatening or stand out. If asked why I was in the neighbourhood, I could say I was looking for a lost dog. The bone would as good as prove what I said to anyone. Everything in place, I locked the car and walked past the store.

The sign just read cleaning supply, and the window displayed several steam cleaners and large floor waxers. There was only one man inside; he was seated behind the counter watching a small TV. I continued down the street before circling the block to get back to the store.

The door had no chime, so Uncle Guy didn't look up from the television until I was a few feet away. I had already figured out he was alone in the showroom and spotted the only exit, a closed door ten feet away from Guy behind the counter, when my presence was acknowledged. He snorted loudly and swallowed whatever he moved in his throat before he stood. He was a fat man with huge features. His large nose and heavy cheeks were peppered with blackheads. They were so large I thought I could work them out with needle-nose pliers. He wore a golf shirt with maroon pants that were hiked up high on his waist, making his torso look short and wide. The golf shirt must have once been washed with the pants because it was dyed an uneven light pink. Guy wore it without an undershirt, and the tight top showed every roll, nipple, and imperfection. He looked at me through dirty greasy glasses and spoke. His breath was stale from smoking.

"I'm losing a fucking bundle on AC Milan here."

I didn't respond so he continued — beginning with another snort. "What can I get for you?"

I looked around the store, making a big production of it so Guy's eyes followed my gaze. "What have you got that takes out blood?"

Guy snapped his eyes back to mine and looked at me, suddenly unsure. "What do you need to take blood out of?"

"Dom told me you're the man to see about cleaning a place right. If you know what I mean." My voice didn't come out weak or wobbly like a liar's; it came out smooth

— a conspirator's voice with just the right amount of malice.

Guy leaned back in close — smiling now. "What the fuck did you get into, hunh? What's the blood on? Wood? Carpet? Concrete?"

I looked down at the dingy brown-carpeted floor. "Carpet," I said. "Old worn-in carpet."

"If the carpet's old, you'll have to do the whole floor or else someone will know the one spot was cleaned. How long has the stain been on the floor?"

"Not long," I said. "Not long at all."

Guy paused for a wet snort. "I got a couple a steam cleaners that will take anything out as long as it's fresh. The size you need depends on the size of the stain. How much blood is there?"

"There's gonna be a lot of blood, Guy," I said as the side of my mouth started to move. The grin formed on my face and it did to Guy what it used to do to me when I saw it on my uncle's face. He was unsettled, unsure of what to make of it. It occupied him while my right hand pulled out the rubber bone.

"Gonna? What the fuck you mean gonna? How much blood is there, stunad?"

I didn't answer. I was too busy swinging the bone up from my hip. I swung it like an overhead tennis serve. The bone arced back as I made a split-second pause in midair, and then shot forward with my arm's change in direction. The hard rubber pounded into the fat face, popping the swollen nose like a water balloon. Blood went all over the thin pink shirt and counter. Guy put two bloated hands up to his face. The fingers, thick like rolls of toonies, tried to hold back the sudden gush of blood.

I took a handful of the greasy, thinning hair on the top of his head and pounded the hands with the bone. I beat them away from his face and began swinging at his short, fat, tyrannosaurus arms. Guy's limbs began to writhe over his head, simultaneously trying to protect his head and avoid the blows. I had to climb over the counter to keep a hold on him. I kept swinging, moving up the flailing arms back to his head. His arms soon became too beaten to cover up his head, and there was nothing to protect the dog toy from cleaving skin away from the browbone. The strikes beat him down to the floor behind the counter.

Guy bled into the carpet and began to sob. The sound was like a child crying in the night. They were heavy sobs accompanied by heavy snorts. The sobbing meant I did my job right. He was hurt, bad but not out, or worse, dead. I didn't waste time checking on him; he was a man who had covered up countless beatings and worse. Why did he deserve better than he gave to his customers?

"Help! He's having a heart attack! Someone call an ambulance!" I didn't know if Guy's son Denis was in the store or not, but if he was I had to get him out and keep him off balance. Paolo said Denis never left his dad alone, and I had to rely on Paolo's intel. Sure enough, the door behind the counter opened and a man emerged from the back room. The man was a younger replica of Guy. He was not as fat, not as greasy, but equally ugly.

"What happened?" he yelled as he approached.

I put panic in my voice. "He grabbed his chest and collapsed!"

Denis reached his father. "His face! What happened to his . . ." Staring at his battered father, Denis never saw the bone coming; it hit him in the temple and shut him down.

I patted Denis down and freed a gun from a holster at his back. I also pulled out his wallet and cell phone. I stuffed the wallet and phone into my already full pockets and tucked the gun into the front of my pants.

I left father and son on the floor together while I locked the front door. I pulled the blinds down over the windows, dimming the room. I freed Denis's gun from my waistband and thumbed back the hammer as I moved behind the counter and checked Guy and Denis. Guy still sobbed and gurgled on the floor. His beaten arms tried to rise off the floor to his face but repeatedly failed. Denis was still out, his temple darkening from the impact of the sap.

I moved through the doorway into the next room; it was lit by too many fluorescent lights, and the aggressive glare hurt my eyes. The room had huge crates and boxes along the wall connected to the storefront. The crates and boxes were labelled with different brand names that I'd heard of before. The boxes looked heavy and likely dampened all sound coming in and out of the room. Denis probably had no idea anyone was out front with his father until he heard me yell. The rest of the room didn't belong at all. There was a flat-screen TV with surround sound set up around two huge leather couches. Behind the couches sat a large desk with a computer terminal. The TV was tuned to the same soccer game as the TV behind the counter. A darkened bathroom was through a doorway beside the desk. A quick check showed me that the bathroom got none of the expensive upgrades that the other room got. It was white, or it once had been. There was piss on the floor, and the seat was up. I backed out of the empty bathroom, careful not to touch anything.

All in all the back room was small, but it looked like what it was — a comfy clubhouse for thugs. I turned off the television and walked back out front into the dimmed sales area. Both father and son were still down on the floor together. I walked past them to the first vacuum I saw — a huge industrial model. I pulled the power cord out of a large retractable spool on the back. The cord came out and retracted with a loud snap when I let it go. I tucked Denis's gun back in my pants, freed my knife, and unwound the cord until there was none left. I cut the power cord into three-foot sections and threw them over my shoulder. When I finished I had six sections in all.

I righted Guy's chair and yanked Denis up to his feet. He surprised me, surging up with the momentum of my pull. He rammed me hard into the counter and tried to drive me over it. I lowered my body and forced him back. I didn't bother pushing his shoulders. I put two hands on his face and shoved — making sure to dig my thumbs into his eyes. His head lurched away, but his arms kept pushing against my body. I drove forward harder with my thumbs and felt his arms start to slacken. His hands stopped trying to shove me over the counter and began to pull at my thumbs. His rage and anger about what I did to his father made his bulky body impossible to hold. He shook his head free from my grip, moving it back and forth like a dog shaking a rat. With my hands loose, he stepped back, maximizing the four feet of space between us.

His eyes looked red and livid, and his wild right hook proved what they were telling me. Denis was fighting for his life, but his sloppy style and heavy breathing let me know he had lost his head and was just running on rage. I wasn't like him. My chest rose and fell evenly; the surprise of his playing possum had long worn off. I stepped into his wild hook, making the fist no real threat at all. The hook turned into a grab once it couldn't hurt me with bone-on-bone blunt force. Denis pulled my body closer, forcing me into a headlock. He was surprisingly strong for someone who looked so out of shape. My neck compressed under his damp armpit. The pressure wasn't immediately threatening because my right hand guarded my throat, but the choke would eventually slow me down. My fist punched repeatedly back and forth like a piston, battering Denis's ribs, but the folds of flesh and his loss of sanity made everything I did ineffective. He cranked harder on my neck and rested more of his weight on my frame. He was screaming in my ear as he tried to wrestle me down like a steer.

The pressure, combined with the hot, smelly air under Denis's arm, began to make it hard to breathe. I gave up punching and grabbed a fistful of his right pant leg. Holding his leg in place, I moved my right hand away from protecting my neck. The pressure surged higher without my arm pushing against the choke, and my vision began to dim around the edges as the air was forced out of my throat. With the last seconds of consciousness I had left, I pulled Denis's gun from my waistband. In one motion, I cocked the hammer back and put the barrel of the small revolver against his shin bone, right between knee and ankle. I pulled the trigger and felt the smelly vise release my neck. Denis was still screaming, but the pitch was higher now that he was on the floor with his shin bone splintered.

The sound of Denis's screams gave his father strength, and Guy surged off his back onto his hands and knees. Before he could get any higher I cut him off, pistol-whipping him on the top of his head. The greasy hair on his scalp offered no protection, and his body slammed to the floor.

Denis still screamed while he clawed at his leg. He tried to cradle his leg, but each time he attempted to touch his shin his hands flinched away as though he was touching fire. I walked past him and righted the chair. I looked at it for a few seconds and realized two things: the chair would no longer help me do what I needed to do, and I had to shut Denis up. In this neighbourhood most people would ignore screaming, especially those who knew what really went on in the back room of the store. But if I let Denis do enough yelling, eventually someone would call for help, either from the cops or from the boss, Dom the Bomb. I picked up one of the pieces of extension cord and walked back to Denis. I flipped him over and looped the cord around his face like he was a horse. I put my foot in the centre of his back and pulled with two hands. The cord fought against his strained lips and teeth until it gave up a little slack as it slid into his mouth. I choked up on the cord and held it in my left hand as I pulled Denis's left arm behind his back. I stepped on the wrist with my heavy boot and heard him whimper a little louder against his gag. With the one hand immobilized, I turned back to his bit and tied it off behind his head. Once it was tied, he could no longer scream — he was only able to grunt through his bit as I finished tying him up.

I kept my foot on his left arm and pulled his right hard behind his back. I put a knee on his spine, brought Denis's hands together, and tied them with extension cord, feeling no remorse for his predicament. His feet followed without a fight. Any movement of his feet would have meant excruciating pain for his damaged shin. Once he was restrained, I flipped him over and looked at the gunshot wound. Blood leaked through the hole the bullet made, and the fabric of his pants tented on jagged shards of bone that were pushing out from around the wound. I took another piece of cord and tied a tourniquet around Denis's leg four inches below the knee. The knot was tight, and within a minute the blood loss was already tapering off. I used the rest of the cords to tie up Guy; his battered, unconscious body offered no resistance.

The situation was a disgrace. I spent years meticulously planning jobs to go off without a hitch, and here I was knee-deep in a father-son massacre. What I had done inside the cleaning-supply store was everything I wasn't; it was crude, blunt, and out of control. I was being used and it was only the beginning. I let the anger wash over me for ten seconds before forcing it back down. I had to force my teeth to unclench when I noticed the grinding was an audible sound inside my head. Inside I knew that the state of Denis and his father was not because of me. I had no real intel on either man or their boss. All I had was some names on a slip of paper. Paper provided by a man who was teetering on the edge. Paolo forced me to move on two men I had never seen at a pace he knew to be reckless. He was not the calculating man I had known anymore; he was a grief-stricken uncle and a vindictive mob boss. Both sides of his personality were pushing me hard to find out who took Army and Nicky. When I did, I wasn't sure who would be taking revenge. As bad as the situation was, it would only get worse unless I became the one controlling the chaos. I had to make sure this clusterfuck never came back to bite me or Paolo, because if it did, it would bite Steve and Sandra too.

With his father still out, Denis had nowhere to look except up from the floor at me. I pulled the recorder from my pocket and turned it on.

His sweaty, pale-white head began to shake back and forth. "No," was the message I got.

"I'm going to take off the gag and we're going to talk," I said.

His head shook harder, pleading with me to leave the gag on. He grunted at me and bucked on the floor. His teeth gnashed at the cord in his mouth as though he was trying to hold it in place. I used two hands to roll him onto his front. Denis squirmed harder, trying to move farther away from the counter — farther away from me. I grabbed the cord tied around his head and pulled his skull from the floor with it. His body arced up in an armless upward-facing dog while I slid the knife in sideways between the cord and his hair. The knife was razor sharp, but I still had to saw at the cord for a couple of seconds to get it off. The sudden release and lack of hands sent his head straight to the floor. His skull impacted like a melon falling in the produce aisle. The sound was flesh, bone, and teeth breaking and bruising.

Denis moaned into the floor until I rolled him again.

"No!" His word came as a loud mumble. He was not afraid of me. He was afraid of his boss. Paolo said Bombedieri was still working — just under the radar. Whatever he did, it scared Denis more than being tied up with a hole in his leg. He wouldn't talk into the tape recorder. He wouldn't unless I became the scariest thing in his universe.

"We need to talk," I said.

He shook his head hard, almost banging both sides of his face on the floor with the frantic side-to-side motion.

"Denis, talk to me and I leave. Don't, and I stay here with you and Dad. I don't like soccer, Denis, so I'll have nothing to do here but work on you. I just want you to tell me a few things so I can leave."

He stopped shaking his head and looked me in the eyes. "No," he said.

I stared back at him and said nothing. I grinned at his smashed face. He looked at my face and he found in it something unsettling because he stopped staring at me and began to strain his neck in the direction of his father, looking for help that would never come.

I stepped past the bodies into the sales area. I walked past the different floor cleaners until I came to a display of bleach, the bottles stacked in a pyramid on the floor. I hefted one of the bottles off the top of the pyramid and checked the label. It was concentrated bleach. I turned the bottle further and looked at the warning label. Words like "severe" and "damage" popped out at me. The label also warned of sensitization if the bleach hit damaged or broken skin.

I carried two bottles behind the counter and set them on the countertop. Denis had shimmied himself past his father to the doorway leading to the back office. I grabbed him by the leg and dragged him back beside his father. I put one heavy boot on his ankle and stood on it with my full weight. For a second I felt his bones move and crack; it was like standing on thin ice. He screamed even after the cracking stopped. I contemplated gagging him again, but the screams stopped when I began unscrewing the bleach bottle.

"No, no, what are you going to do?"

I didn't answer. I pulled the safety seal and hefted the bottle up with my left arm. My work in the city had once left the arm useless, but I had worked to make it strong again. The months of work it took were hell, and once I finally became whole again I got dragged back to the city so the whole process could start over again. Denis wasn't responsible for that, but he was part of the machine that was. He could point me in the direction of the people who set the wheels in motion. A fact that made it easy to tilt the bottle.

The milky liquid fell from the mouth of the bottle to the ruined pant leg. At once, the cotton fabric of the pants began changing colour, becoming lighter and whiter with each splash. The liquid soaked the pants and flooded in the hole left by the bullet. Denis's legs shook hard trying to move away, but his ankle was pinned under me. His restraints made any momentum he could have gained impossible. All he could do was scream as a half bottle of bleach hit his legs as though it were some sort of chemical waterfall.

His screams woke his father, and the old man looked on in horror while he struggled against his restraints. Denis's eyes were wide in his ugly face. The bleach burned the skin, but worse than that, it made the wound more sensitive. The bottle had not lied about sensitization — every nerve ending in the wound was on fire because of the bleach.

I put the bottle down and looked at the newly pale pant leg I had created. Denis was all screamed out; his mouth just silently opened and closed. His face had gone more pale, and his bloodshot eyes bulged out, unblinking. I was now the terrible centre of his universe. Bombedieri no longer existed. I was all he could see.

I picked the bottle up again with my left hand and the recorder with my right. I tilted the bottle halfway and felt the liquid settle at the edge of the mouth.

"Tell me about what Bombedieri is into, Denis."

"Oh, God. Oh, God."

There was still some residual fear of Bombedieri in Denis's mind. I let a little more liquid hit his leg to wipe it away.

Denis screamed before he started talking in fast, rambling sentences. "He runs the neighbourhood. He controls everything: drugs, gambling, girls. He even pays off the cops."

"More," I said. "What has he done recently?"

"He killed those bikers. He shot them. Him, and Tony, and Phil, and me. We shot those guys in their car and left them there in the field. No one knows it was us, but we did it."

I didn't know anything about bikers, but the information was important. Information could be used more places than MasterCard. It also proved that Denis was involved with everything his boss did. Denis didn't sit on his hands in the back room all day, he was a player. If Bombedieri was involved with Army and Nicky, Denis would know.

"What about kidnapping?" I said.

"What? No. We don't do that. There's no money in it. Oh God, my leg is on fire. It's burning."

I splashed more bleach on the leg, and Denis screamed through every octave. I shut the recorder off and asked my last question.

"Bombedieri take Armando and Nicola? Is he working an angle?"

The pain moved to the back of Denis's mind for a second as he looked up at me. He realized he had no idea who I was or why I was there. He probably thought I worked for the bikers he crossed until I asked about Army and Nicky.

I splashed more bleach and asked again. "Did your boss do something to Armando and Nicola?"

"No! Jesus, no! He hated those two, but when we told him we wanted to hit them for all that shit they pulled he said no. He said we couldn't do it now. That it would fuck up our operations in the neighbourhood. He said they were off limits."

"You sure?" I said as another splash hit the pale pant leg.

"We didn't touch them, I swear. We were too busy with the bikers to deal with those fucks. Please, no more. Please. Please!"

I cued up the tape and played it back. As the tape played, I stopped being the centre of Denis's universe. I was slowly eclipsed by Bombedieri. "You're going to run," I said. "I'm gonna pass this tape on, and you don't want to be here for the fallout. You and your dad need to get out of here and never look back. You gave up your boss, and there's no way he'll let you off for that. Especially after the bikers get their copy."

"I'm dead, then," he said, exhausted.

"Your life here is over, but you're not dead. Not yet

anyway. You two need to go, and go far."

I wiped the bottle with my sleeve and left out the front door. Denis didn't move as I walked away from him. He just lay silent on the floor, letting shock set in, temporarily taking him away from his death sentence.

CHAPTER THIRTEEN

I used my elbow to open the door as I left the cleaning-supply store. Once I was outside, I casually stopped to look at the hours of operation. I pulled my sleeve over my hand and wiped the door handle as I leaned in to see the hours posted on the glass. I nodded my head as though the opening and closing times pleased me, then walked away from the store to my car.

Denis had to run. He and his father had to clean up the mess I left and get as far away from the city as they could. The tape I had on Denis was more deadly than a cruise missile. If the tape got out, which he believed it would, there would be nowhere safe in the city for him. I counted on his fear, on the utter terror Bombedieri put in him, to send him running.

I walked up the street to the car, watching every window and alley. I had seen no one watch me go in, but I knew that fact didn't cover me going out. As I moved up the street, I passed a kid sitting cross-legged on the pavement playing a guitar. His black leather case was closed beside him, and I had to step over the neck of it as I walked past him on the sidewalk. The kid didn't look up at me while he played; he kept his red head down. He didn't even pick up the pace of the song to earn a donation for his effort and skill. He just played his song, oblivious to the world.

I saw my car up ahead, and on the trunk sat two men in their early twenties. Instinctively my hand began to swing closer to the front of my pants as I walked. I still had Denis's stubby revolver tucked in my waistband. The two men, if you could even call them that yet, were in faded ripped jeans and old unlaced high-tops. They were at an age where they weren't children anymore, but at the same time they could never be considered men. The only word that came to mind was "punks." One was blond, and his hair stuck out from under a sideways baseball cap. The hair was meticulously placed so that it shaggily hung over one eye. The other had long, greasy black hair that made it hard to see most of his face. His long beard covered everything below his nose so the only bit of skin I saw was a small patch of forehead. Both of the men looked pale and strung out. Their knees bounced on the bumper to an irresistible, soundless, chemical-induced beat. The dark-haired one shoved the blond with a heavily tattooed elbow as I got closer. Both looked at me. My mind raced as my eyes met the two pupils I could see peeking through the mess of hair on each punk's face. There was no way these two were after me. They were white punk-rocker kids — about the farthest thing from Paolo and his organization — and yet there they were, waiting on my car.

I stopped three cars away, my hand near my belt, and looked at the two punks on my trunk. Before I spoke, something pulled at my mind. The guitar player had his guitar case closed. He wasn't there for money, so he had to be there for something else. The guitar was no longer being strummed — I couldn't hear it — but I could hear singing. I recognized the words as being from an old Ramones song.

"Beat on the brat. Beat on the brat. Beat on the brat with a baseball bat. Oh, yeah . . ."

As the song behind me grew closer, I watched the two punks on my trunk tense their shoulders and squint their eyes as though they were about to be hit with a snowball. Just before the second "oh, yeah" of the chorus I tried to roll forward. My head and shoulders started the roll, but the baseball bat that smacked across my lower back ended my attempt.

I fell to my knees and fought to pull air back into my body as the two skinny kids jumped off my car using the bumper as a springboard. I watched the two pairs of feet approaching as I listened to the singing continue behind me. The guy had moved ahead in the song and was laughing as he sang, "What can you do-oo." The singing was terrible, but it bought me the seconds I needed. I got a quarter of a shallow breath and rolled off my hands and knees onto my back. My right hand groped for the pistol and yanked it free from my waistband. I had the gun out and moving to the centre mass of the red-headed punk standing over me, but the ball bat to the back did the trick. I was slow on the draw, and the kid above me had time to swing the bat low, connecting with the snub-nosed revolver in my hand. The gun went off when the bat connected with it, but the shot went wide.

"Holy shit! He's got a gun," one of the voices behind me said. The voice was not full of fear; it was equal parts laughter and excitement. "Give Dirty Harry an encore."

Another swing didn't come. The punk with the bat had stopped his attack. His face was down, and he was checking to see if he was shot. I knew there was no way I could pull the other gun from the tight pocket on my thigh without getting brained by the bat, so I kicked out instead. The toe of my heavy boot found the soft spot between the redhead's legs. He cringed and then crumpled in on himself, collapsing to the pavement.

I got to my feet just as two sets of hands began laying into me. The punches were wild and everywhere at once.

"Come on, Dirty Harry, make my fucking day," one voice said as a fist hooked into my ribs.

A kick to the side of my leg wobbled me, and I heard, "Oh ho, that was lucky. I was lucky that time, Harry. How lucky you feel now?"

It was as if I was being swarmed by bees with knockout power. I covered my head and tried to weather the storm, but a punch to my exposed and injured back changed that. The blow to my back straightened my body as though an electric current was shot through it. The two punks behind me saw me straighten, and they began to focus on the back of my head. I bent forward and kicked out behind me like a barnyard mule. My foot found something solid, and I heard a grunt. I staggered forward, still covering my head, trying to get away from the three attackers.

A hand grabbed my ankle, and I looked down to see the red-headed singer holding on to me with two hands. I kicked out with my right foot, and my boot split his eyebrow open. The blow was enough for me to get my feet free. I kept staggering forward until I was shoved face first into a parked car. The punk with the hat and the bangs had done the shoving; he was still untouched and ready to go. I pushed off the car and flung myself backwards into the punk's body. Once our bodies connected, I leaned forward and then slammed the back of my head into his face. The impact had me seeing stars, but I was free to run

MIKE KNOWLES

again. I looped around the car and began stumbling up the street towards my car, using the other parked cars on the street as a buffer to separate me from the three punks. I fumbled for my keys and managed to get them out five feet from the bumper.

"Batter up, motherfucker."

I heard the words in conjunction with the feeling of the bat. The impact hit me in the back again with such force it made my teeth rattle. I bounced to my knees, not even feeling the pavement. The car keys fell from my fingers, and I pitched forward. I saw the pavement accelerate towards my face then lurch to a stop and reverse away from me. Three sets of hands stood me up and began beating me. Fists pummelled my face and guts all at once.

"Get his ass into the van."

"Ah, come on, Mickey. My fucking stomach hurts from that asshole's foot. Let's use his car. We were gonna jack it anyway. This way we don't have to come back for it. Harry here won't mind. His feet are burning up anyway from all that kicking. Ain't that right, Harry? You got a real *hot foot.*" With the last two words, the kid with the beard, that I had kicked, stamped down hard on my foot with his heel. The boot absorbed the impact, and I didn't feel a thing. I screamed out anyway to avoid a second blow somewhere softer. The impact of the foot stomp on the steel toe must have hurt the punk with the beard. His worn-out Converse high-tops would offer no protection against that kind of activity. He took my scream for gospel as he shifted his weight from one foot to the other. There was no way he was going to try for another stomp.

Mickey, the redhead the punk with the beard was talking to, pressed a hand to his damaged eyebrow. Out of the corner of my eye, I got a good look at him. He was tall, six feet five at least, with red hair — real red, not dyed. His arms were large but not muscular. He was probably stronger than most people simply because of his unnatural size. He had thick leather bracelets on his wrists and a pair of dead eyes that gave his face a sort of zombified look. He seemed to manage talking without moving his lips. He sighed. "Fine, fine, whatever. Let's just get this fish back to the whale. You two put him in and drive him back in his piece of crap. I'll get my guitar and follow you back in the van."

"Righteous, let's get some fucking drive-through on the way back. I'm jonesing for a Frostee."

"Gonzo, you are taking him straight back. We can't fuck this up. You heard what the whale said."

"Ah, come on, Mickey. Me and Ralphy just want a snack. Look at Ralphy's mug, that asshole cracked the side of his face. He probably needs to get his head in a cast. He needs something cold, something soothing, something chocolate."

Ralphy stopped adjusting his sideways hat and tried to speak. He failed on his first attempt and brought his hand to his face in pain. Through the hand cupping his face, he finally got out, "Yeah, dold."

"Plus I don't want to eat that shit the whale puts out. I hate that Italian shit. I want a burger with extra cheese."

Ralphy nodded and forced a "mm-hm" through his hand.

Mickey shoved Gonzo and Ralphy hard, and they almost dropped me. "Get him back to Domenica's. Then we can eat. Got it?" He poked Gonzo hard in the sternum with the top of the bat for emphasis. Blood trickled down his face from the wound I gave him with my boot. Mickey felt the blood and swiped it away with the edge of his hand.

"All right, all right, shit. Just wanted to eat is all. You're so fucking critical. Fucking guy from Oasis was like that, and look where they are now."

MIKE KNOWLES

This seemed to really piss Mickey off. "Oasis is a shit Manchester band. Up on stage singing about champagne supernovas and shit. They champagne super suck. Now get his ass in the car before I make *you* ride in the trunk."

Mickey's anger spurred everyone into motion. I was thrown backwards against the bumper and the rear of the car rammed into my lower back. The blow crumpled me to the ground, pushing the small specks of gravel on the pavement into my knees. Mickey's tall frame loomed in front of me, and I swung for it. The punch got no help from my back, making it less than a weak swat. The other two laughed at my offence, and each took a handful of shirt and collar. One of their shaky hands lost its grip on my coat, so my ear was used to pull me off the ground.

"Hey Mickey, Harry here kicked me and he messed up Ralphy's face. We should get a chance to get him ready for his ride."

My eyelids fluttered as Gonzo launched his fist into my head. He put his weight into it, and both of us went down. With double vision, I didn't know which of the six men around me to grab on to. Twice I got it wrong before my hands found the one that had hit me.

"Get the fuck off me, Harry!" Gonzo shrugged my weak grip off and got back to his feet.

Ralphy stood over me with his identical twin. He cradled his cheek and grunted twice through his pursed lips at the tall redhead. The redhead seemed to understand the grunts and replied, "Yeah, fine, but make it quick."

Ralphy began to stomp me in unison with his twin. I tried to block out one, then the other, until I figured out which one was really Ralphy. The stomps weren't that hard, but they were fast and rhythmic.

Gonzo was bent over the side mirror adjusting his hair and beard. He stopped twirling his greasy hair to laugh.

"He's playing your tune, Mickey."

Mickey looked at me hard and then began bopping his head to the tune of the feet bouncing off my ribs. He began to sing along with the beat; the song was near the end of the chorus. "Beat on the brat with a baseball bat. Oh, yeah. Oh, yeah." There was a pause and then two more stomps: "Oh, oh."

Mickey looked around the street and stopped thinking the beating was so funny. "All right, all right, get him in the car. The whale wants him alive and like ten minutes ago."

Once again I was in my car, but this time I landed on the fabric floor of the trunk on top of the spare. The shocks bounced with my weight, and the lid closed before I could even turn over.

As soon as the lid closed, I began to feel my body. Nothing was broken; the kids had cracked a rib at worst. Ralphy had sacrificed power to show off his musical talent on my midsection. Two teeth were missing from the side of my mouth where Gonzo had hit me, and one of my eyes was swollen, but it didn't matter — I couldn't see in the dark anyway. I knew the double vision would pass quickly, probably before the trunk lid opened. I was beaten up, but my head was clearing. The three punks had not frisked me after they saw the gun. I was alive in the trunk, and still armed.

It was hard to breathe with my rib cage resting on the spare tire. I adjusted my body in the cramped space until I found the least uncomfortable position. The fact that I wasn't frisked meant the three punks had probably never done this type of thing before. Another clue was their urge to stop for drive-through with a live body in the trunk.

Once I figured out that my back wasn't going to get any looser in the quarters I was in, I worked the nickel-plated revolver I took off Johnny back on the island out of the concealed thigh pocket of my pants. I got the gun free as the car roared to life and jerked away from the curb, causing my back to spasm again. I bit my lip to stifle the scream and thumbed back the hammer on the revolver. I stayed in my cell, in the trunk of the car, sore, angry, and holding a dead man's gun.

CHAPTER FOURTEEN

The ride in my own trunk was rough and bumpy. I could have pulled the glowing knobs that released the back seats and gotten out, but then I would have had to kill Ralphy and Gonzo. I fought down the urge for revenge. It was tough to do — like swallowing a jawbreaker — but it had to be done if I was going to learn who wanted me delivered to them.

I felt a heat in my face that I knew was not a result of the beating I had taken. What I had known deep down was just proven to me. I was out of shape. Not physically. I wasn't hard anymore. Too much time away without the constant buzz of danger and paranoia had let a mental atrophy sink in. There were parts of me that had not seen use in two years. I had controlled the situation with Denis and his father, but I hadn't trusted my gut on the sidewalk. There was a time when on impulse alone I would have taken apart the singer on the street and disappeared before anyone knew what was happening. But I ignored the itch in my brain and walked past the punk. I ignored his panhandling in the wrong kind of neighbourhood, and his closed guitar case. I had gotten lazy, and it had cost me. I was riding in my own trunk to my execution.

Everything that had happened was my own fault. I had ignored every lesson my uncle had ever taught me. I had not planned what would happen inside the cleaning-supply store before I walked through. I just moved on two dangerous men because I was pushed hard by Paolo. I should have slowed things down and made a move when I knew everything would be covered. I could have walked into an empty store, or worse, an early meeting. I realized that being pushed was no excuse for what I had done in the cleaning-supply store. Being locked in my own trunk had a way of forcing me to reflect. The trunk was a cramped, smelly wake-up call. I remembered what I already knew. I had to make everything work for me; I had to be the one pushing the action, or I would constantly be on defence. No matter how good someone's defence was, they always get scored on, and this kind of game was sudden death.

I figured that whoever pulled me off the street had to be involved with Paolo in some way. How else could they know where to pick me up? What I couldn't figure was: who would use three greasy kids as heavies? They didn't look Italian, and they didn't sound Russian. Someone hired these three and they knew doing so would cover their tracks. I was only sure of one thing — they came at me outside the cleaning-supply store. That meant they weren't with Bombedieri; his men would have moved on me inside. Denis was right: Bombedieri had nothing to do with Army and Nicky disappearing.

Once my breathing had slowed and my heart rate was down, I opened my eyes and looked at the blackness inside the trunk. There was nothing useful to pick up — the car was cleaned the day I took up fishing. All I had was the gun, knife, and electronics. The bone sap was still in my pocket, but it would be useless when I didn't have the element of surprise.

I shifted around in the trunk and pulled the sap, phone, and recorder out of my pockets. Whatever I was going into, I didn't want to give up a safe phone and the only information I had gathered. I pulled up the covering on the floor of the trunk and put everything underneath, in the back corner. It felt lumpy when the cloth cover was put back on, but it would be a good enough hiding spot.

I was double-checking my work when my body was thrown forward. We had stopped. The engine stayed on, and the trunk lid stayed closed. After a minute, the car inched forward, only to stop again. After another minute and another lurch, I heard Gonzo yelling up front. His words were muffled, and I couldn't make out who he was speaking to until I heard another voice up front make a whiny grunt. Gonzo yelled louder than before, and I caught the words, "Oh, oh, and two Frostees too! I need two chocolate Frostees!"

We were in the drive-through. Gonzo and Ralphy had a body in the trunk of a stolen car and they were stopping for burgers. I had to bite my tongue to keep from screaming out in anger. Three complete idiots had taken me off the street. The humiliation hurt worse than the beating did. My self-pity was interrupted by more voices from the front seat and more lurching. I listened to the incoherent exchanges until the car peeled away and I was thrown to the back of the trunk. The car went through a series of tight turns until it settled into a long acceleration. We were back on the road, and the smell of greasy food was wafting through the seats into the trunk.

The smell of the food made my stomach turn and made it hard to keep my mind on the blow to my ego. The part of my mind that was beyond such trivial matters became louder and took over. I decided I would let the kidnapping play out until I had no other choice. If they tried to search me, I would have to make it tough in order to conceal the revolver in my waistband — no small feat when I was outnumbered three to one.

I closed my eyes again, ignored the nauseating smells, and resumed my deep breaths. I let the harsh rocking of the car sway my limp body rather than thrash it around. I opened my eyes periodically, looking at the glowing seat release knobs. They looked like PacMan. I stared at the plastic and thought of my uncle. He taught me to play the video game and to stay one step ahead of the ghosts, to play their game better than they ever could. I remembered the feeling of control I had when I could finally manipulate the ghosts, when I could lead them instead of just run from them. Being in the trunk made me mad, being in the city made me furious. My jaw had been tense for two days as I dealt with the problems of the past, problems I thought were dead. In the trunk, over the noise of the city, I heard my uncle laugh. His words hit me then, and I remembered what I had buried in my mind while I worked the ocean. "Don't get mad. It's a weakness someone will exploit. You need to be able to think without connection to your emotions." It was advice I learned in a coffee shop over an out-of-date video game. But I learned to live the advice, and I stayed out of trunks. My uncle would only give me change if I played the game his way — the right way. And now, stuck in a trunk, I realized I had stopped playing his way. I wanted more quarters so I could get out of the trunk. I wanted to play another round because all at once I remembered everything. I realized that my jaw had loosened on its own for the first time in two days. It loosened because I was grinning in the dark. The grin was

MIKE KNOWLES

something that years on the boat couldn't touch or wear down. It came from deep inside and it was part of me, a part I couldn't deny or dull no matter how much I thought I could, a part that breathed air for the first time in years in the stale, cramped confines of the trunk.

I swayed in the trunk for five more minutes until we jammed to another stop and the car became silent. We were there. I closed my eyes and covered my face, making myself look weak and hurt. I stayed there for two minutes, until I heard a conversation through the metal lid.

"I can't believe you never tried to make your own Frostees, Ralphy boy. Everyone has tried that shit."

"Dou did?" Ralphy's mouth was messed up from my head.

"Of course, bro. Chocolate, ice cream, and milk. I even threw in Nestlé's Quik to make it extra chocolatey."

"And dow das it?"

"I used too much milk. The blender exploded all over the kitchen. My mom was super pissed."

"Dour mom had do dlean it?"

"Man, I was so high I just fell asleep at the table. I was gonna do it, but I just dozed off for a second."

"No wonber we could never practice at dour place."

The trunk opened, shining light through the spaces of my bent elbows over my head.

"Wake up, you fucker. This Frostee is killing Ralphy's mouth 'cause of you."

I groaned, and they both swore before stepping back to set their Frostees down. "Seriously, everything he says is all fucking garbled. He sounds like he has marbles in his mouth."

"I dan't even daste it. My deeth durt doo much."

"See? What the fuck was that. 'Dan't even daste.' If he was our lead, I would have fucking left your ass in the street. Fuck the whale and what he wants; he's not more important than the sound. Count your blessings, Harry."

They each reached in and together pulled me out of the trunk hard, straight onto the pavement. I stayed limp, making it more of a chore. They muscled me vertical, each of them using an arm to hold me up. Once I was standing, they both bent at the waist to pick up their Frostees. It would have been easy to kill them both while they concentrated on their dessert. Ten minutes ago, I would have. But it was a new game, so I just let them fuck around. Another set of hands slapped me on the back of the head — Mickey was back. I groaned louder in response.

"I told you not to stop for fucking food."

"Come on, Mick. We worked up an appetite with Harry here. We had the munchies."

"Deah, de munchies."

"Hurry up and get his ass inside."

Mickey walked ahead, not bothering to help his two partners. Ralphy and Gonzo had to pull my limp body behind Mickey while they tried to eat the last of their food. I dragged one boot along the ground and let out low groans every ten seconds. The groans were met with laughter or a "Shut the fuck up, Harry." Every now and again, I rolled my head and took in my surroundings. I was in a poorly paved parking lot outside a squat building. There were several cars near the rear of the lot, old models, all rusted and dented. I was dragged to the back of the building to a door guarded by two large dumpsters. The back door had no handle, no peephole: it was faceless. One of the dumpsters had the word *Domenica's* stencilled on the side. I had no time to try to decipher the word. The smell of rotting food wafting from the two dumpsters filled my nose and told me all I needed to know.

Nothing on the list Paolo had given me included anything about a restaurant or the name Domenica's. Bombedieri, Perino, and Rosa were not in the food business, according to the information I was given. Someone outside of the people I was dealing with knew I was back.

Mickey banged on the door with his palm when we caught up to him. He didn't offer to relieve Ralphy and Gonzo of my weight, even though they were obviously struggling. The sound of the knock echoed in the parking lot. We waited for a minute until a dishwasher in a soaked, filthy white apron opened the door. Immediately steam and loud techno music hit me; it was like a pipe had burst at a busy nightclub. The dishwasher said nothing to the three men. He just ran outside to hold the door. He averted his gaze as I passed by, refusing to acknowledge the hostage he had no intention of helping.

I was muscled through the door by the two weakening punks. My dragging foot caught on the step into the building and tore the leather on the toe of the boot. The damage was worth the "oof" that came from Ralphy's and Gonzo's lips as they almost fell. They swore and dragged me on, too tired to hit me anymore. The kitchen was busy with people in white coats chopping and dicing vegetables. Like the dishwasher, none of the kitchen staff looked my way. Beyond a swinging door that served as an entrance to the kitchen was a dance floor. It was dark and buffed to a high gloss. In front of the dance floor was a stage piled with heavy amplifiers and other equipment. I groaned and looked over my shoulder to the rear of the restaurant. Behind me, through an empty doorway, were tables in a darkened dining area. Domenica's was more than a restaurant — it was some kind of club. I was dragged to the centre of the dance floor and held in place by my captors.

"Leave him there. Let him go. Take your hands off him," a voice behind me said.

I knew right away who the voice belonged to. I knew of only one person who repeated himself that much. The three punks called him the whale, but I knew whose place I was in. Domenica's was Julian's club.

I didn't hear his footsteps. He glided into view from behind me, a mammoth tripod. Julian walked with help from a cane. I knew that the cane was my fault. I had hit Julian with a stolen truck two years ago in an attempt to stay alive. I had gone through Julian, Paolo's number two, to get back the information I had stolen from the Russians. I had hit him the hardest way I knew how and I hadn't killed him; I just slowed him down — permanently.

Gonzo spoke up. "Boss, he's pretty fucked up. We did a number on him outside Bombedieri's. If we let him go, he ain't gonna be standing. You want us to put him in a chair?"

Julian stood in front of me and my two young punk crutches. "Let him go. Take your hands off him. Turn him loose."

Ralphy and Gonzo looked at each other then at the giant tripod in front of them. I felt them shrug and then chuckle. At the same time, they unhooked their arms from mine and stepped away. I didn't fall. Instead, I stood up straight and looked Julian in the eye.

"Quite the number. Real professional work," Julian said, looking at me but speaking to the two who had just been carrying me.

"He was out. He didn't make a peep the whole ride. Not even at the drive-thr —" Gonzo stopped himself.

"Boss, we did it just like you said." Mickey took over and began speaking for the group when he saw things getting away from Gonzo.

"Go do your sound check. Set up. Get ready for tonight," Julian said to Mickey in a quiet, stern voice.

Mickey understood the threat underneath Julian's tone and pulled Gonzo and Ralphy away to the stage. They may have called him the whale on the street, but the three punks knew what Julian was and wouldn't dare oppose him in his presence.

"Let's go," Mickey said.

Once I was able to stop faking injury, I did my best to take in everything around me. Julian was ninety-nine percent of my surroundings. His bulk and rage filled the room like a silent gas ready to ignite the air. He periodically leaned on the cane for support as though his massive body might teeter over at any moment. The black suit he wore was heavy, and it hid his physique. The size was still there, imposing and terrible, but I couldn't tell how much of the size under his coat was still muscle. His hair had a bit more grey to it, and it was heavily gelled, giving it the appearance of constant wetness. There was also a smell emanating from his huge frame. It was cologne and sweat. There was so much body to cover that the cologne could not hope to cancel out the body odour; it could only tinge the smell of sweat. The nights of hot kitchens and dance floors did not agree with Julian. His suit held on to the smell, and it had probably become unnoticeable to Julian. The smell probably remained unknown to him because everyone around him would be too terrified to mention it.

Without a doubt, Julian was still a force, but he was no longer the immovable object he once had been. He instead seemed to be an irresistible force driving those around him, but who was it he kept around him?

"What's with the greasy kids, Julian?" I asked.

Julian looked at me without saying a word. I watched as veins on his forehead woke and began to pulse at the surface of his skin. "The kids," he finally said. "The kids, they do jobs for me. Things I can't do for myself. They're my hands. You should understand that. You were someone's hand once. Someone who did jobs for someone else."

I understood what Julian had inside his restaurant. He had his own version of what Paolo had. Julian had organized three outsiders to do his work for him. Three strung-out punks who were loyal, vicious, and, most important, deniable. No one would expect that the three punks worked for Julian. Even if they admitted that they did, no one would take their word for it. Julian had his own restaurant and his own agents. He was like a photocopy of Paolo. Everything was similar, but just a little less perfect than the original.

"I'm no one's hand anymore, Julian."

"Bullshit!" he roared. "What the fuck are you doing here if you're not someone's hand?" He seethed in front of me; his massive chest forcing the fabric of his suit farther and farther off his chest. "Maybe you're just his dog, then. His pet. An animal. Dogs come when you call and they love you more when you're mean to them because they got it in their head that it's always their fault. That your problem, Wilson? You his old dog hanging around for a kick, a punch, a beating?"

Static from the amplifiers interrupted Julian's rant.

"Goddamn it!" Julian bellowed over the noise.

"Sorry, boss," Mickey yelled back.

Gonzo yelled to Ralphy, "Harry's name is Wilson. That's even dumber than Harry." Ralphy laughed and then held his cheek, suddenly in pain.

"Fucking pieces of shit. They aren't good for much, but they got me you, didn't they? Outside of Bombedieri's. Why did Paolo bring you back from that tiny island to go there?"

My eyebrow raised a centimetre.

"What? You thought no one would find out? That old man has everyone watching what he does. Everyone is waiting for him to slip up just a little more. He can't handle the Russians. He can't even keep his family in line. But you know that, don't you?"

I said nothing. Julian was prepared to talk, and I wanted to hear every word he had to say.

"That old man is falling apart. There's no one left to hold him up. His little *figlio* ran away, and all at once he was blind."

"What about you?" I asked.

"Oh, you know about me. I was better than you ever were. But after your little stunt, I was useless. The old man thought there was no way I could keep him safe with one hand on a fucking stick all the time. I'm lame, a cripple, a fucking gimp. I got set up with a place to retire. A gift for all my years of faithful service."

"Seems like a nice place," I said.

"It's a fucking dive. All I get is dirty kids who are into loud music. No matter how hard I try to get people in to eat, I end up with a full dance floor of dirty kids and an empty dining room. This place is like a curse. I renovate it, rename it, change the menu, but no one will come in unless there's loud shitty music. This is my reward, my legacy, a building full of shit. Shitty people and shitty music."

As if on cue, static electricity erupted again from the amplifiers. Julian turned and yelled, "I swear to God, Mickey!"

"Sorry, boss."

"How did you know I was back?" I said.

Julian laughed and at once, he seemed to forget about the cane and amplifiers. "The guy Paolo sent after you, Johnny, he's my guy. My *paisano*. Most of Paolo's guys are after what he let you get away with. He can lock me away in this hole like a fucking family embarrassment, but there are others who remember me. Johnny told me he was going out east to find you. Johnny said Paolo was sending him because he was loyal. You see? That old man doesn't even know his own people now. But Johnny did his job. He found you and brought you back."

"No," I said.

"No?"

"I found him. Then I came back."

Julian's eyes narrowed, and I could see we were almost through talking.

"Check, check," Mickey said into the mic.

Julian's cheek twitched.

"Check, check, one, two," Mickey said again. Gonzo hit the drums in a loud semi-rhythmic beat.

Julian's eyes fluttered.

An electric guitar came to life, and Julian exploded. He turned to the stage and screamed, "Shut that stupid shit up, you worthless fucks! Turn it off!"

At once, the three stopped what they were doing. Their hands froze, and their jaws went slack. Julian stopped yelling and said, "What?"

"This," I said.

CHAPTER FIFTEEN

The barrel of Johnny's revolver, the revolver I had brought back across the country, was out of my pants and pressed firmly into Julian's neck. Two inches of the barrel disappeared into neck fat, showing me how far Julian had fallen from what he used to be.

Julian roared at the band, "You didn't frisk him?"

Mickey spoke into the mic. "We took his gun from him on the street. Then we knocked him around. He was out cold on the pavement. We didn't want anyone to see us so we just put him in the trunk. He was out cold, so we thought it was safe."

"Boss, he never made a peep at the drive-through. He was out," Gonzo piped in.

Mickey shot Gonzo a look that shut him up. They both turned their heads to look at their boss. Julian's shoulders heaved up and down as though he were growing in size.

"Enough," I said. "How did you know where to pick me up?"

Julian didn't turn to look at me; he glowered at the

band while he answered my question. "What? You think I wouldn't know why he brought you back? What you were here to do? I knew exactly what that old man would do. I always know what he'll do."

"Did you know he'd put you out to pasture here?" I asked. I took his silence for a no. "Who took Armando and Nicola?"

"I don't know. I'm not in the loop anymore. No one runs things by me and no one officially tells me anything. I got contacts who remember the favours I did for them, so I hear some things, but those new guys Paolo brought up when he put me away on the shelf — them I got nothing to do with."

"So you think it was someone in Paolo's circle?"

"I don't know. I do know that no one would have dared try anything like this when I was around. No one. They knew who to fear. Now, no one has history. No one fears. No one respects. No one knows what family is about. They're all out to make money."

"Army and Nicky weren't involved in the business. Paolo said so."

Julian chuckled. The movement of his massive frame caused him to wobble on his cane. "You can't make money if you can't maintain your reputation. Those two assholes said some dangerous things. Someone would have to respond."

"Why? Those kids are connected."

"Are you stupid? You got rocks in your head? Did you learn nothing in all the years you spent with us? It's like I just told you — no one's connected anymore. Paolo has to promote new guys all the time. Family's not important anymore. How could it be, when people are getting replaced every day? Money and power are the new family. There are a lot of people who wouldn't blink at killing two loudmouth kids — no matter who their uncle was. Nothing holds these young killers in line anymore. They're like wild animals."

I eased the gun out of Julian's neck, and his tensed shoulders relaxed. He just finished a sigh of relief when my leg kicked his feet out from under him. Julian tried to stabilize himself, but his cane was no help to his heavy body already on its way to the floor. He hit the glossy dance floor with an impact that I could feel through the soles of my boots. Julian didn't waste any time on the ground; he rolled onto his back and began to sit up, using his hands for support.

"Why did you come after me again?"

Julian looked angry and unafraid from his spot on the floor. "You look at me and you gotta ask why? I owe you. I did this for payback. Revenge. Vendetta. You left me a gimp. You cost me everything. I'd give anything to do the same to you, to take away from you everything you have and leave you broken, so that everyone knows I'm more than some crippled owner of some dive. I'm not this, I was never supposed to be this. You should be this."

Out of the corner of my eye, I saw Gonzo moving behind his drum kit. Ralphy was moving his eyebrows up and down, trying to instruct his friend in some sort of idiot code. Mickey stood still, guitar in hand, towering over the microphone stand in front of him. His shark eyes, sunken in his pale face, were watching me. His face was blank, as though he was watching television, a rerun he had seen before that could now barely hold his interest. I moved the gun away from Julian's chest towards the amplifier to the right of Gonzo. I pulled the trigger and heard the boom followed by the screech of the damaged amplifier. Gonzo and Ralphy jumped; Mickey didn't even twitch.

Ralphy fumbled with the amp cord, finally managing

to pull it free to end the deafening squeal. With the cord loose in his hands, he began to giggle. Gonzo joined in. The insane laughter must have been infectious because Mickey's deadpan face began to twitch into what he must have thought was a version of laughter.

I watched them laugh. They looked like hyenas holding musical instruments. I tilted my head, never taking my eyes off the animals on stage, to look at Julian. He was biting his lower lip as he looked away from the stage at something only he could see. I bent at the knees and picked up the cane that had fallen from Julian's hands when I knocked him over. Gonzo and Ralphy still howled while Mickey contributed a bit of shoulder shaking to his smirk.

I held the cane in my hand and was surprised by its weight. The cane was a solid piece of wood with a polished sphere of metal at the top. I knew the cane was custom made for Julian because few people would have the sheer strength to use something so heavy as a walking aid. I looked at the band members, who were still lost in their hysterics, and let the gun hang loose at my side. I stared at Mickey and watched him laugh his creepy laugh. I felt my lips pull, and I matched his smirk with my own grin. His shoulders stopped shaking as hard, and his smile dimmed a fraction, changing his expression into something more confused than entertained. I flipped the cane over with a toss and lifted it above my head. I let it pause in midair before I sent it hurtling down onto Julian's ankle.

"Jesus!" was all Julian could scream before the cane hit the ankle again. Each time I brought the cane down on Julian's ankle, Mickey's smile moved down another millimetre. The cane bounced off the bones in Julian's leg at first. Each impact propelled the metal sphere back up into the air like a happy child on a trampoline. But each blow generated less and less spring as the skin bruised and the bones began to shatter. I hit Julian's ankle long after he passed out. I crushed the bone and kept going. Gonzo and Ralphy caught on to what I was doing and they stopped laughing, only to start up again while watching me work. I stopped when Mickey was done smirking.

"You want to sing me your song again?"

Mickey didn't answer.

"No? No tune to sing? You see this right here," I said, pointing to Julian's soft unconscious frame. "This happened before. You could call it my greatest hits. I bump into you three again, it won't be like it was on the street. There won't be a song. You won't see me coming — you'll feel it."

Mickey still didn't move. His mouth hung slightly open, and his shark eyes stared back at me unblinking. I dropped the cane with a clatter and brought the pistol straight up at Gonzo. The revolver's humourless black eye stared at the laughing kid, unimpressed. Gonzo stared into the barrel and stifled his giggles. He looked into the gun's one eye and then into both of mine. He whistled the tune from *The Good, The Bad, and The Ugly* and then began laughing again. I walked to the stage stairs, keeping the gun's eye on Gonzo. Mickey watched me approaching without saying a word. Ralphy had gotten another case of the giggles and said, "Oooh, scary," through his swollen mouth.

I stopped three feet from Gonzo and said, "Give me the keys."

Gonzo patted his pockets and shrugged his shoulders. "Sorry, man, they must be in my other pants." He and Ralphy began laughing at his joke. These punks were something new. No real crew would use such violent, immature addicts. Whatever they spent their free time pushing into their blood had changed them. They didn't look at the world like everyone else. They were manic, psychotic snowflakes. They had just witnessed their boss getting beaten and had wound up with a gun pointed at them and they couldn't stop themselves from giggling. It wasn't nervous laughter, either; it was the laughter of things in the dark. It was the laughter of predators. They were too young and stupid to understand that there are things that even predators have to learn to fear.

"Check again."

He patted his pockets and lifted his arms in an "I don't know" gesture. I sighed and looked away. Gonzo turned to Ralphy and began to laugh again. "My other pants. I don't even own these — they're yours. Remember? I lost mine after that show."

Ralphy laughed a bit too hard; his hand flew to the cheek I dented with my head.

"Hot foot," I said, remembering how funny they thought it was outside my trunk. Gonzo looked back, still laughing, but now half puzzled about my words. I let him think about it for a second, and then I pulled the trigger.

The revolver sent a piece of lead straight through the old Converse All-Star Gonzo was wearing. The shock and pain cut through all of the chemical giddiness. "What the fuck, man? What is your problem?"

Ralphy stood up behind his drum kit, but I waved him down with the gun. Out of the corner of my eye, I saw that Mickey had not moved an inch.

"The keys," I said.

"Fuck! They're in the car. I left them in the ignition."

I walked away from the three kids and Julian's unconscious body. Everything hurt, but Julian would be worse. I was alive and back in control. If I could have, I would have laughed like Ralphy and Gonzo.

CHAPTER SIXTEEN

The keys were in the car as promised. I took the Volvo out of the restaurant parking lot without stopping to retrieve the electronics I hid in the trunk. I left the restaurant and watched each street sign fly past the windshield as I tried to get an idea of where I was. At an intersection, I saw that I was on Duke Street. A sight that made a bell ring in my head. I pulled out the sheet of paper that contained Paolo's information and looked at the addresses. Luca Perino worked out of a place on James Street — which was less than a minute away. I couldn't believe it. I was right where I needed to be.

Paolo's info put Luca Perino inside Ave Maria — a little shop that sold Catholic religious items. A huge portion of the city was Italian Catholic, and religious stores were a common sight throughout Hamilton. The colossal statue of the Virgin Mary I saw in the window of Ave Maria as I drove by told me the shop blended in just fine in the city. The shop would repel most people. Almost everyone preferred stores that catered to their vices rather than their spirituality. Those that did venture in off the concrete would either know about the shop's dual identity and not mind — seeing it as commonplace in the community — or the customers would be so pious they would not even think to notice the blasphemy taking place behind the counter.

I drove slow in the right lane eyeing the rows of cars on both sides of the street. I was looking for one vehicle in particular, according to Paolo's intel — a white Cadillac Escalade. The Escalade had been a mob staple since its inception. It was a sort of moving billboard broadcasting the fruits of criminal success to the community. A white Escalade was a bit different than the standard mob black, but I figured an up-and-comer would want to be part of the trend and at the same time identify himself as special.

The car wasn't on either side of the busy street, so I used Main Street to circle around to Hughson, which ran behind the shop. I drove slowly up the less busy street and stopped in the parking lot behind Ave Maria. There was no Escalade, only a rusted Dodge Shadow parked in an employees-only space along the side of the building. There were two other employee spots vacant, something that didn't sit well with me. A shop this small and this specific would never have more than one employee working at a time, two tops. Of the prospective employees, there was no way that they all were drivers. Stores like this would not offer enough cash to pay for a car, and the deeply religious women who typically worked behind the counter were usually unmarried or widowed, making them lower-income wage earners and thus frequent bus passengers. One of the two vacant parking spaces was much bigger than the other. The hand-painted lines were a bit wavy, but they were clearly designed to contain two cars of different sizes. No one painted parking spots behind stores like this — it was too much trouble. Someone had gone a long way to ensure that a really big car got a permanent spot. I was sure I could figure out what kind of car fit inside the painted lines.

I reversed the Volvo and backed into a spot that offered a view of the parking lot from a safe distance. No one in the parking lot I was watching would be able to see me inside the dark interior of the car. From Ave Maria, the Volvo would look like just another car taking up a free space on a side road. I unfolded the paper Paolo had given me and took the time to really look at the information on Luca Perino. Perino was in charge of his little world around James Street. His number two was a man named Marco Monaco. The paper gave me the address of the shop, physical descriptions of everyone involved with the business, and a phone number. With the car stopped and no one in sight, I decided to call the number and see what happened.

I eased myself out of the car, being careful not to twist my ribs more than I had to. I opened the trunk and pulled back the fabric covering on the floor. Underneath a spot of blood left by my face while I travelled in the dark was everything I left. I took everything in the trunk and got back into the front seat. I powered up Johnny's phone and dialled the number.

"Ave Maria," a pleasant female voice answered. She sounded older than her twenties but younger than her fifties. Beneath her words rose the sounds of hymns from a sound system in the store.

I decided to take a shot at it. "Ah, yes, hello. My name is John Clark, and I work for the city of Hamilton."

"How can I help you, Mr. Clark?"

"Well, you see, this is one of the rare calls I make that I enjoy. One of the calls I make where I can actually help you. You see, the city reassessed your area last year, and somehow in the shuffle we neglected to adjust your property taxes. As a result, we owe you some money."

"Well, that is a first. The city paying money to the people instead of the other way round." Her voice sounded very chipper. She was genuinely happy about my lie.

"I need to come in and have some papers signed before I can make out the cheque. Let me check my computer . . . I would need the signature of a Mr. Monaco. I have him listed here as the owner."

"Mr. Monaco's not the owner, Mr. Per —" She trailed off into a quiet murmur as her mind caught up with her mouth.

"Hello? Miss?" I sighed, knowing she was still on the line. "Darn phone. Hey, Jerry, my line went dead again. Can I use your —"

"No, it didn't. I'm here. I'm sorry, I just got confused. You're right, Marco is the owner."

"Is that Mr. Monaco?"

"Yes, he is." Her voice was chipper again. She had decided that although Luca Perino was in charge, his name was probably off the official books. After all, he was a big wheel in the mob. The woman on the other end of the phone wasn't one of those ignorant religious patrons of the store — she knew the score.

"Is he there now? I would love to get this taken care of right away."

"I'm sorry, he's not usually in until six o'clock."

The dashboard clock read 4:00. Julian had held me up, but not enough.

"I will have someone walk over the papers then. I'm off at five," I said.

"I'll let him know you're coming. He'll be so pleased. It's not every day that someone gets money back from the city."

"No, it's not," I agreed. "Thank you so much for your help."

"God bless you, Mr. Clark," the woman said, and then she hung up.

I closed the phone and shifted to put it away in my pocket. As I arched my ass off the seat to get at my pockets, I felt nothing but a searing pain through my torso. Every part of me burned, and although I was sure there were no broken bones, the pain made me question the health of my organs. I got the phone in my pocket without screaming. I kept my body off the seat so that I could stash the digital recorder in my pants too.

Once I was back in the seat with a new coat of cold sweat on my brow, I leaned over to the glove box and pulled out the cord that came with the digital recorder. I spent a minute testing the cord in each hole in the device before finally managing to fit the cord into its corresponding hole. I had at least two hours before Marco Monaco, Luca Perino's number two, would pull into his small parking space. There was no way I was going to spend two hours with my rapidly cramping body inside my car. I needed to move and loosen up. I got out of the car, taking everything except the rubber bone with me. I checked the parking sign on Hughson, making sure the car wouldn't be towed or ticketed where it was, and walked away.

I walked down Hughson until I hit King Street. King was second only to Main in its possession of legitimate businesses. The stores that lined the roadway were, for the most part, legitimate, successful retailers. The places that worked under the radar and off the books were all on the veins that led into the major arteries of commerce like Main and King. I walked the street in between the numerous bodies of pierced kids and unwashed adults. I passed a strip club and several pizza places, while I scanned the street for an Internet café. I found one on a side street just off King. I walked into the deserted café and paid up front for thirty minutes.

I opened the web browser and pulled up a free e-mail account I kept. I plugged the digital recorder into the computer and listened to the chime of hardware recognition. I clicked the Attach icon and pulled the file off the digital recorder. Once the transfer was complete, I addressed the e-mail to myself and sent it off. The e-mail was in my inbox by the time I had the recorder back in my pocket. I cleared the web browser three times and shut the computer down before I got up to leave.

I walked out of the café without another word to the employee behind the counter and followed my nose onto King Street towards a pizza place I passed on my way to the Internet café.

The pizza place sign just read "pizza" in big, bold, neon letters. The walls of the tiny restaurant had a repeating phone number stencilled all over them with the words "Two for One" added in anywhere they would fit. There was a counter directly open to the street that everyone had to wait in front of for their food. I didn't like being exposed to the entire street, but rusting in the car like the tin man was not an option. I waited patiently and used the constant flow of young women in slutty clothing as an excuse to scan the crowds around me. I was not a man hunting the mob; I was a hungry pervert, like the rest of the men in line.

I ordered two slices of pepperoni pizza and a Coke and waited under a minute for the lukewarm Italian food to get to my hands. I took the food with me across the street to Gore Park.

Gore Park is a small patch of grass in the heart of the city core. It could be walked around in under three minutes, but no one ever did it. The park was like a safari of human suffering. Homeless kids, derelicts, and people on the verge of becoming either were in constant supply. No one stared into the park when they were at the red light on King Street —

it just seemed like an invitation for disaster. Seeing everyone look away from the park made it almost magnetic to me. It was a rare find in the city. A place where a person could be invisible while being completely visible.

I walked past the homeless until I found a vacant rock. The pizza bag offered little resistance as I tore through the grease-soaked paper. The right side of my face, on the other hand, put up the fight of its life. I had lost teeth from the side of my jaw, making chewing difficult. I spent half an hour using my tongue to mash the pizza against the left side of my mouth before I swallowed. The Coke's acidity burned the empty sockets in my jaw, so I didn't drink often.

I ate to the point of physical exhaustion. The food felt good in my stomach and it was quickly taking the edge off the pain I felt. I tore the last of the food into bits and fed it a piece at a time to the gulls that had slowly been surrounding me while I ate. The gulls made me think of the island. They made me remember what it was like away from the city. The island wanted me back, but nothing could pull me away. Paolo had anchored me here, tied me to the city I tried to leave behind. I looked at my hand as I threw the last piece of pizza to the birds. My hands were no longer good for tying off knots and setting lures. I was back to what I had been. My hands were gnarled mitts again — useful for beating and stealing. Each uncomfortable breath made the island seem more like a fantasy and the city a painful reality. Suddenly, the greasy pizza felt like a stone in my stomach, and all I wanted was to be moving.

By the time I slid back behind the wheel, it was 5:15 p.m. I looked through the windshield and noticed that the little space was full. A black, two-door Mercedes was in the lot beside the beat-up Dodge Shadow. Marco was early for work.

I didn't want to go in and repeat what had happened at

the cleaning-supply store. There wouldn't be any bleach here, and I wasn't interested in beating up a female employee of a religious store unless I had to. I knew I wasn't going to heaven, but I wasn't so far gone that I was going to start doing the devil any favours. I needed to get Marco out of the store without raising suspicions, so that I could deal with him alone.

My body stayed still in the car as my mind raced over the possible ways to handle the situation I was in. I no longer felt pushed to act right away. I didn't feel apprehension or anger. I searched my mind for the feelings, but they weren't there anymore. The sickness from the pizza had evaporated, and I was left in the car. I was focused without connection. I was my uncle's nephew again.

After two minutes of thought, I arched off the seat and endured the pain of retrieving my cell phone. I dialled Paolo, who answered on the fourth ring.

"I need something," I said before he could even finish his greeting of, "What?"

"I told you not to call unless you had good news. I told you I would get you some incentive if you needed it. Is that why you're calling? To test me? I can make a call right —"

"It wasn't Bombedieri," I said.

"How do you know?"

"I asked the right people the right questions the hard way."

"And you think they'd tell you anything? You have gone soft."

"I asked real hard. I know I'm right, and you know it too."

"How do I know?" he asked.

"You brought me back into this because you know what I am. I'm a grinder, I'll find out everything. Bombedieri is only concerned with his turf and bikers."

"What did you do? This can't come back on me." Paolo sounded mildly panicked. He instantly knew I had done what I said because I mentioned the bikers. Bombedieri's move against the bikers must have been a real hush-hush job.

"It won't. Now, I've given you your good news. It's your turn to give me something."

"Give you — give you — You work for me, remember?"

"I'm out of the loop, and things are going to have to start moving faster."

"Why?"

"Never mind why. It's nothing," I lied — deciding to leave Paolo in the dark about Julian's misfit crew. Julian would send them after me again. He'd have to; his pride would accept nothing less than me dead in a painful way. He had known I would go after Bombedieri; he would figure out Perino, too, once he was conscious and lucid again. I had to settle up before he was back on me. Knowing I had dealt with Julian and that he was already informed about why I was in the city would put Paolo into damage control. He would have to erase all evidence of everything he had me do. That would include erasing me. He would correct his mistake by killing me, and he'd use Steve and Sandra as bait to get the job done.

"*Figlio*, don't you lie to me. What happened?"

"Everything is working like clockwork. I just don't want anyone to have the chance to start talking to one another and compare notes. Time has a way of ruining things."

Paolo seemed to buy my story. "What do you want?"

"I need you to call Luca's number two."

"Marco? Why?"

"Tell him something happened at Bombedieri's and you need eyes and ears at his place. Tell him you can't get a hold of Perino, and you need someone you trust over there to investigate."

"Then I'm involved. I told you I can't be involved. What the hell is wrong with you, *figlio?*"

"Nothing you say will hurt you. You're the top guy in the city. You have eyes everywhere, so you easily found out something was wrong at Bombedieri's. You don't know all the details and you need to find out. All true so far."

"Stunad! When you grab him, he'll figure it out. You're not thinking."

"He won't tell anyone anything. In ten minutes you'll call his cell phone again, and he won't answer. Then you send someone else in his place. Marco will get there eventually, but he'll never mention a word about why he was late — not even when you punish him for slacking off."

"Punish him? Why would I want to —"

"If anyone didn't do what you said right away, what would you normally do?"

Paolo was silent on the phone. His silence was like the sound of a basketball swish. I had scored a point on the old man. I was thinking ahead of him.

"You just do what you would do to any disrespectful hood. Even when you come down on him like a head-on collision, he won't say a word."

"Why not?"

"I'll make sure it's in his best interest to not say a thing." I hung up the phone, forcing Paolo to act, because there was no other alternative on the table. He wanted to know who was behind Army and Nicky's disappearance and he had no one else he could use to find out. Paolo had to work with me until he got what he wanted.

Minutes later, the back door opened, and Marco Monaco ran out with his keys in his hands. He was going so fast that he almost missed me leaning on the wall beside the back door. He ran two steps ahead of me before he looked over his shoulder to confirm what he must have thought he saw. He had a hard time seeing me behind the rubber bone swinging at his face.

arced the bone high over my head and brought it down like a volleyball spike. Monaco, a small man with ratlike features, didn't make a sound in the split second it took him to notice the bad situation he was in. His mouth formed a small O just as the blow connected above his ear. Then his eyes crossed and closed. His knees went next — all at once.

The keys Marco was carrying were on the pavement beside his body. I bent at the knees, to save my back, and picked up the keys and Marco's wrists. I dragged Marco to the passenger side of his car and opened the door. I bent and lifted the little man's unconscious frame into the car, but it was next to impossible with the shape my back was in. I left gangster on the ground while I went around to the other side of the Mercedes. I lay across the seats and used my upper body to pull Marco's torso into the car. When he was half inside, I got out, went around to the passenger door, and bent to lift his feet in. For a second I thought I wouldn't be able to straighten, but I managed to climb my way to a vertical position using the car as support. With Marco's feet inside the car, I quickly pulled his laces from his leather shoes. I knotted both laces together and used them to tie Marco's wrists behind his back. The rope was thin, but it looped the bony wrists enough times to make a solid binding.

Once Marco's wrists were tied, I got in the front seat beside him. I freed the gun from the holster on his hip and glanced at the Glock 9mm before putting it under my thigh on the seat. The Glock was something I knew. It wasn't flashy and it wasn't the most powerful handgun out there; it was just accurate, reliable, and dangerous.

I started the car and clicked the cigarette lighter down. I leaned in the seat and breathed deep. I tried to relax my back with each breath, but it was slow going. The metallic click of the lighter brought me back to the here and now.

Riding out another spasm, I looked over at the man beside me. His skin was tinged olive and his hair grew straight up from his scalp in a finger-in-the-light-socket sort of way. I looked from the welt on his temple to the acne scars on his face. This little man was part of the puzzle. He was either innocent or guilty, but either way he knew something that I needed to find out, and I was going to grind it out of him.

I clicked the lighter down again and reached over to Marco. I grabbed his bony nose between my thumb and forefinger like grandfathers do when they say, "Got your nose." In my case, I actually tried to rip it off by twisting it and pulling it away from his face.

Marco came to just after I heard a wet snap.

"Oh my God! My nose! Stop it! Stop it!"

I stopped and watched as Marco tried to cup his nose only to realize that his hands were not responding. He leaned forward, head against the dash, and strained against the bonds. I pulled the lighter and pushed it behind Marco's ear. The circle of metal burned through the hair growing on the side of his neck and sent his body reeling back off the dashboard.

"What the fuck was that? What did you just do?"

He finally looked at me, and then at his gun. He stopped talking when he saw his Glock pointed at him. His ratty buck teeth bit his lower lip, and his eyes watered. "Wh — what do you want?"

I clicked the lighter back in its space. "Marco, you need to fill in the blanks for me."

"Blanks? What blanks?" He was already calm. The blow to the head and the burn already seemed distant as he clearly spoke to me.

"I want to know about Armando and Nicola."

Marco looked at me for a few seconds, then he smiled. "That's why Paolo called me. I thought it was weird that he called me to check on Bombedieri. I said to myself he's probably got dozens of people he could send, but he tells me to go. Why me? But who says no to the boss's boss? Man, I shoulda known. So, how'd you figure out it was Luca P. who did it?"

I didn't let the surprise I felt show on my face. "Everybody talks," I said. "I just found the right people."

"You're lying."

"Why do you say that?"

"Because people don't talk about this. Luca P. did it, but he didn't talk about it to anybody. He doesn't even know that I know."

"If people don't talk, then how did you find out?"

Marco let out a sigh and looked around.

"No one's coming," I said. "If they do, I'll just drive us away, so spill it. All of it."

When he said nothing I pulled the lighter again and

showed it to his eye — up close.

"All right, all right, shit. I was just thinking, but I'm done. Okay? I'm gonna tell you everything, okay? So knock it off with the lighter."

I sheathed the lighter. "Why so co-operative? Shouldn't you put up a fight?"

"That's what I was thinking about. Way I see it, Luca did something on his own — without me. I'd stick with him on that if it was a job. I ain't no rat, but what he was into . . . He killed Paolo Donati's family. That's a death sentence. I'm not dying for something I had no part in."

"How do you know it was Perino who took the boys?"

"I saw them the night they disappeared."

"With Perino?"

"No, I saw them here. Luca gave me and the other boys the day off. That never happens. But hey, who says no to a day off? I slept in and spent the day playing soccer. At dinner, my mother tells me she lost her rosary."

"You live with your mother?"

Marco looked annoyed. "Don't judge me. Just listen. She lost her rosary and she tells me she needs a new one so she can pray to the Virgin for my Nona, who's in the hospital. So we get into this big fight 'cause I tell her I'll get her one tomorrow when I go to work, but she says, 'What if Nona dies tonight?' So I finally cave in and I go down to the store to get a rosary. I got a key and I know the security code. It's no big deal. But when I pull in, I see the parking lot is full. Luca's car is there with two others. The BMW that was there was Army and Nicky's."

"How do you know?"

"They had a personalized licence plate on the car so everyone knew who owned it. No one else is riding around with DONATI on their bumper."

"Who owned the other car?" I asked.

"I don't know. It was a big van, blue, and the bumper was rusty. I knew what those kids said about the boss online. Add that to my day off and there was no way I was going in there. I got the hell away."

"What about the rosary?"

"I got a friend to loan me his mother's."

"You ever ask Perino about what you saw?"

"I know what I saw. What good would asking about it be?"

I nodded my head as I pulled the tape recorder out of the cupholder and turned it off.

"Oh shit. You were taping me? You were taping me. I told you everything. You don't need a tape. Come on, you don't need that. I'm dead if that gets out."

He stared at the electronic device as though it were a black widow spider. The recorder was much deadlier than any arachnid. There was no anti-venom that could save Marco from the tape; it was a death sentence pure and simple. The rat-faced gangster watched me put the recorder in my pocket. He knew his only chance of survival hinged on what I did with the recording in my pocket.

"Where were you going just now?" I asked.

"I was told to go check on Bombedieri. That's where I was going."

I pulled the knife from behind my back and watched Marco's eyes open wide. I used the barrel of his Glock to force his head against the dash while I cut the shoelaces and put away my knife. When he sat up, I patted the pocket holding the tape recorder.

"In about two minutes, people are going to hear what you told me. Understand?"

He nodded.

"If you were lying, you just did it to the wrong people.

If you were telling the truth, you might have just earned yourself a promotion."

Marco actually smiled at me, letting me know he told the truth.

"Get yourself to Bombedieri's and do whatever you were told to do."

"I can go?"

"In a minute. Get out of the car."

I took the keys out of the ignition and got out while Marco stared at me with a puzzled look on his face. When his door finally opened, I closed mine and walked around to the back of the car. Marco closed his door with his foot while he rubbed his wrists. "Fucking shoelaces hurt, man," he said as he came to meet me behind the car. He shut his mouth when he saw the gun in my left hand, away from the street, pointed at his belly.

I threw him the keys. "Open your trunk," I said.

"Why?"

"I'm going to give you your gun back. Then you're going to get moving. The gun is going in the trunk. You can get it out when you're gone." I turned the gun around and held the barrel in my right hand.

He nodded, accepting what I said.

"You're really just gonna let me go?"

"Marco, you're set to inherit this whole place. The boss needs to keep the system working. He needs someone who knows the ins and outs. You and me are done. You got a job to do now, and so do I. By tomorrow your paycheque will be much better; so will your parking spot."

He popped the trunk with the key fob and lifted the lid straight up with his right arm. He turned his head to me and laughed, still holding the lid. "I hate this fucking spot. I had to get this car 'cause it was one of the only ones that would fit. If that ain't bad enough, I gotta put up with the boys always asking me if my girlfriend loaned me her car for work."

I looked inside the trunk and was happy with what I saw. "You won't have to worry anymore, Marco." He started to laugh until my left hand grabbed a handful of his shirt. I swung the Glock by the barrel and the butt hit Marco in the centre of forehead like a hammer. He stiffened and began to fall back like a hewn tree. My handful of shirt guided his falling body into the trunk. The open cavity sucked him in head-first.

CHAPTER EIGHTEEN

"You won't be taking over, Marco. You're just at the start of a long night. Some people are going to want to talk to you, so you just need to sit tight." If Marco heard me, his limp body didn't show it. I pulled his keys off the pavement and fished the wallet and cell phone he was carrying out of his coat. My pockets were full enough, so I threw the phone and wallet in the back seat. Marco didn't move while I opened and shut the door. He didn't even stir when I pulled his hands out of the trunk. I laid his wrists across the edge of the trunk twice, the second time pulling more of Marco out of the trunk so that his weight wouldn't drag his hands back into the trunk again. Once the small hands were resting on the lip of the trunk, I checked the parking lot. No one had come out since I put Marco inside his own car. No one was watching, so no one saw me slam the lid down on the small, limp wrists protruding from the trunk. No one saw me hammer the screaming gangster back into the trunk it erupted from, either.

Marco was alive but broken in his trunk. His right wrist, still visible on top of his again unconscious body, was dented. The bone ruptured the skin in a sharp point showing signs of a compound fracture. His chest rose and fell evenly as I leaned in and used my fishing knife to cut the glowing plastic seat release cord at the back of the trunk. The shoelaces would not have held anyone in the trunk for long. Two broken wrists and no seat release would hold him there until someone decided to let him out.

I closed the lid and moved Marco's car out of the small spot into the larger one. There was three feet of space on either side of the car. The little Mercedes would almost be able to open both of its doors all the way without touching another car. The white Escalade would not be able to boast the same feat. It would also not be able to fit into Marco's little space.

I left the two-door in the parking lot and got behind the wheel of my car. I turned the key and backed up twenty metres to a new parking spot concealed by shadows. It was invisible from Ave Maria, but it would allow me to see the Escalade pull in from either direction.

I waited, watching the back door of the store. I wondered when the woman behind the counter, who drove the Dodge Shadow, would leave, and if she would hear Marco alive in his trunk when she left. As the hours clicked by, it was a question that came to be all I could think about. I was debating going back to the Mercedes to help Marco sleep again, or sleep deeper, when the whole idea stopped mattering. A white Escalade took up my entire rearview. The driver's side mirror that showed objects larger than they appeared made the huge Cadillac look like a rolling iceberg. The car drove past me over the curb aiming directly at the huge spot now fifty percent full of

Mercedes. The Escalade was so large that it hid both parking spots in front of it. I couldn't see through tinted glass, but I knew who was inside the behemoth.

The white door opened at the same time as my own. The doors closed in stereo as well. I was jogging towards the tall, thin, olive-skinned man as he shook his head and rifled through a pocket in his coat. As I closed the distance between us, I estimated Luca Perino's height at six and a half feet. He wasn't big — just tall and thin, the kind of thin that mothers everywhere tried to kill with food. His bony shoulders his tented jacket as though the hanger was still inside the fine tailored suit, and his short hair did little to conceal the jutting bones of his skull. His metabolism had probably outrun many plates of food when he was a child.

When I was less than twenty-five feet away, I stopped running and hit the panic button on Marco's key fob. The Mercedes went haywire, and Luca Perino took his phone away from his ear. He walked around his huge SUV to the Mercedes as I clicked the panic button on and off. I could see him five feet from the car as I got closer to the lot. My approach was concealed from view by the huge car, but that wouldn't last. Perino would see me coming unless I gave him something to look at. I popped the trunk using the keys and watched Perino walk slowly towards it. I rounded the bumper of the SUV trailing in Perino's wake to see him bending at the waist to closer examine the contents of the trunk. There was a moment of realization about what was in the trunk, and then the tall man was accelerating to his full height with the phone in his hand meeting his ear at six and a half feet.

"Don't do that," I said, pointing Marco's Glock at the narrow chest of Luca Perino. He had a perfectly trimmed mustache and a vertical strip of hair below his lip. His face had small eyes and a small nose that made him appear childlike. His giant bony fingers, holding the phone next to his ear, ruined the facade. They looked like aquatic predators — all bone and tendon.

"Put the phone down in the trunk."

Luca Perino did not move; instead he spoke. "I remember you. You used to work around here. You didn't have the beard, but the rest of you looks the same." He pointed at me with a sinewy finger. "You look like shit. Little Marco do all that to you?"

I felt my back repaying me for the jog. I extended the gun towards Luca's centre using a hand on the SUV to hold me up. "Put the phone down in the trunk."

Luca held his ground, and his phone. "A lot has changed in the last few years. I've changed. I'm not some nobody thug anymore. I run this neighbourhood for a big name. Maybe you didn't know that. Maybe you should reconsider what you are doing."

He looked confident in front of my gun, towering over the body in the trunk.

"Say the name," I said.

"Who?"

"The big name. Say it."

Luca looked a little unsure.

"Say it," I said.

Luca didn't say a word.

"You don't know me," I said. "The fact that you saw me around doesn't mean anything. Things haven't changed that much from where I stand. The city is still run by one man, and I still have to do what he says. Just like it was before, I'm chained to the old man. He's still the same, and I'm back to being what I was. You, you're new but you're not different. I met people like you before. You're taller, but you're the same."

"Tell me what I am, tough guy."

"You're a big shot running your own turf. You've been doing it a little while now and you're starting to believe the hype. You think you're a big-time player and you're being held back by people with less vision than you. So you, like most before you, did something stupid because you thought it would work out. But it didn't. Just like before, he sent me to find someone like you, and here we are."

"You are really fucking far gone. I have no idea what you are talking about. None."

"Say his name," I said, and I took my hand off the bumper. I stepped towards the tall man towering over the trunk like a scarecrow. His bony hands still clutched his cell phone, but his fingers were whiter.

"Donati," he said.

"Now tell me what you think that old man is going to say when he finds out you took his nephews. Do you think all of those changes you went through will save you? Or will it be just like old times?"

Luca Perino didn't get a chance to answer. A vehicle coming towards the parking lot interrupted us. Headlights shone through the dim evening murk just before the sound of music over a harsh engine caught up with them.

CHAPTER NINETEEN

"Phone in the trunk now," I said as I covered the rest of the space between Luca Perino and me. His huge hands groped for the Glock as it got closer, but they retracted when my steel toe bit into his long shin bone.

The gun was in his ear as I pulled the cell phone free from his tight grip. I threw the phone into the trunk and shut the lid as music grew louder over the roar of the approaching engine. Through the tinted panes of the Escalade, still diagonal in the lot behind the parking spaces, I could make out a pair of headlights. The car stopped, and doors opened and slammed.

The engine stayed on and music poured out of the vehicle. I saw a break in the light streaming through the dark car glass — someone had walked in front of the headlights. I grabbed Luca by the belt, pushing the gun harder into his ear. I dragged him back between the Mercedes and the Dodge Shadow. When my back touched the brick of the building, I used my foot on the back of Luca's knee to put him quietly down on the pavement.

From in between the cars, I could see two bodies at the back door of Ave Maria. In the dim light, I could see that one of the men was tall like Luca, but this one was more solid. Beside him was a smaller figure in a hat that was turned sideways on his head. I could tell without getting any closer that it was Mickey and Ralphy. The two at the door probably meant that Gonzo was the one keeping the music on in the car. He wouldn't be much good for walking in the shape I left his foot in. His presence in the car and the headlights illuminating the lot kept us pinned down.

The car still belted out music while Mickey and Ralphy banged on the back door. They didn't pound on it with any urgency. Ralphy hit the door rhythmically using both hands and the toe of his shoe. Mickey nodded his head with the beat and then murmured something to Ralphy. He started the beat again with greater intensity, and Mickey bopped his head along with the faster modified drumbeat. The punks hit the door with familiarity — it wasn't the knock of a first-timer. Something was off, those doped-up leg breakers should have been scared shitless to hit a mob door like that, but the two of them showed no hesitation or second thoughts.

The door never opened. I figured the woman inside, behind the counter, knew to stay away from the back door and the type of customers who would use it. Her job was the front door of the front, and judging by the closed back door, she stuck to it.

"Why are Julian's guys here at your door?" I said in Luca's ear. He didn't answer, he just shook his head back and forth letting me know he wasn't going to say a word. It wasn't much of a head shake. The gun in his ear made part of the motion impossible.

"Why are they here?"

He just shook his head harder. I didn't need him to

answer. Julian's guys were here because they were after me. They were here just like they were at Bombedieri's. But something nagged at me. At Bombedieri's they were waiting outside. Here, they were at the door, knocking to get in. Who would let those two into a back room that served as a criminal front? Mickey and Ralphy were street level; there was no way they should be high enough on the food chain to get into a neighbourhood boss's backroom office. They would be met on the street by someone under the boss to keep everything separate.

Whatever their reason for being at the door, the whole situation was turning to shit around me. Julian was pushing to kill me and he seemed to know everywhere I would be before I did. Julian was two for two in interference, and I couldn't keep surviving our encounters if my hands were tied. I had the info Paolo asked for. I had Marco on tape explaining that Luca was behind what happened to Army and Nicky. It was half of what Paolo wanted; the other half was deniability. Paolo didn't want anyone to know that he was looking into his own people. He especially didn't want anyone to know he was using me to do it. To keep Paolo in the shadows, and get me out of the line of fire, I had to make it out of the parking lot alive.

With that thought, any instinct to hold off, to try to keep Luca Perino breathing, went out the window. My hands were free of red tape — I was disconnected again, and it felt good. Luca couldn't see me grin behind his back. My face didn't change at all when I pulled the Glock from his ear and buried it in his back — right behind his heart. I pulled the trigger and I was moving before his body hit the pavement.

The music from the car on the other side of the Escalade obscured the shot, but it wasn't loud enough. The shot was sure to bring Mickey and Ralphy over to investigate.

I flattened myself on the pavement and slid under Luca's Escalade. The darkness under the SUV was total, and my shadow disappeared once I was underneath. I held the Glock in my right hand and the Mercedes keys in my left.

I watched from my stomach as two sets of feet walked towards the Escalade. No feet emerged from the vehicle on the street. The music didn't slow down or quiet — it just pumped out a loud, constant drone. It probably made the gunshot non-existent inside the vehicle.

I opened the trunk with the fob when the two sets of shoes got within feet of the Mercedes. I took deep breaths and visualized what I had to do while I waited for their discovery.

Ralphy saw it first. "Holy dhit, Mick! Deck it out, dere's a dody in the dunk. Dhit, man, dere's one over dere too. It's ducking Luca P., man."

As soon as I heard the recognition, I hit the panic button. The feet beside the SUV jumped and moved around in circles as Mickey and Ralphy looked in every direction. I slid out on the other side of the Escalade and ran at the headlights in front of me. The Glock in my hand fired three times, in a quick burst, at the windshield. In half a second, I put a bullet in the centre of the driver's, middle, and passenger's side of what I finally saw as not a car, but a large blue van.

I thought for a second that I was shot while I was in motion towards the van, but each step dulled the pain into decreasing stabs of agony. There was no bullet hole — it was my back reminding me of the beating the three punks in the parking lot had laid on me. The reminder made pulling the trigger easy.

No one returned fire from the van as I crossed the headlights to the driver's side. The bright beams left my vision scarred by a constantly returning bright blotch every time I blinked. Underneath the blotch and over the sight of the Glock, I saw Gonzo slumped against the passenger-side door. I got into the van and had it in reverse by the time Mickey and Ralphy ran out from behind the Escalade. I tried to crouch down while I drove, but my ribs and back made it impossible. I had to lay sideways, my head in the lap of the bleeding Gonzo, as I drove away.

Bullets punched the side of the van as I blindly spun the wheel, shifted into drive, and slammed the accelerator to the floor. Once the metal-on-metal thuds stopped, I pulled myself up, keeping my eye on the sucking sound coming from Gonzo's chest and the gun he dropped to the floor below him.

"You had me fooled, Gonzo," I said. "That fat bastard made me think he was out, and that you and your friends were the only help he could find. Nah, he used you because no one would ever see you coming. Especially not Army and Nicky."

Gonzo let out a low laugh over the sucking sound from his chest wound. He laughed low and hysterically until he died. Two minutes later, I was outside Domenica's.

CHAPTER TWENTY

ulian had never been out. He might not have been Paolo's right hand anymore, but he was still in it up to his ears. Julian was behind everything that had brought me back. Inside Domenica's, on one good foot, was the one person with the answers. He was the owner of the unknown van that Marco saw at Ave Maria. The old me, now behind the wheel of the van, wanted to visit with Julian, and there was nothing to stop me from doing it anymore. I had let him live because there would be more questions if he were dead. Alive, there was a chance he might have talked about Paolo using me, but he'd have proof of nothing, and no one to pin it on, because I planned to be gone by the time he could get anyone to listen to what he had to say. Now he was involved, and it was my job to find out what he knew. For a second, behind the wheel, I was happy to be employed again.

I wiped the steering wheel and door handle with my sleeve and left the van around the side of the restaurant under a burned-out street light. The darkness and the locked van doors would ensure that no one would find Gonzo for a while. The restaurant parking lot was empty except for two cars — a black BMW and a grey Audi. Julian was involved in very dangerous business; he needed to keep everything quiet if he wanted to pull off whatever he had planned for Paolo. After what had happened earlier, he must have given the kitchen staff the night off, so they couldn't witness what was to come. He sent the house band for me, and he must have been waiting for them to come back with my body. Whoever was with him had to be involved with what happened to Army and Nicky. It was too late in the game to be bringing in new people. The reason I had been dragged back to the city was inside the building in front of me.

The front of the restaurant was dark. There were only a few lights on in the back of the building, and they gave off a faint glow under the awning above the front doors. The street light in front was bright enough for people to see the closed sign. I tried the front door, ready to break it open if I had to. The door surprised me by moving inward when I put a little weight against it.

Walking into Domenica's was different the second time around. This time I was able to use the front door and do it with my head up and eyes open. Inside the door, I was met by a small desk. I flipped through the book on top and saw that it belonged to the hostess. Each page was dated and contained a list of times for reservations. No one had ever made any advance plans to eat in the restaurant. The book told me that Julian was right: he had no business at the restaurant — at least not the kind he wanted. The restaurant branched out behind the desk. The dining room was dark, but I could make out tables and chairs set up all over the square room. Behind the tables and chairs was a swinging door and a counter that allowed food to be passed from

MIKE KNOWLES

the kitchen into the dining room. The light at the back of the restaurant was coming from the hallway behind that door. The stage and bar were through an archway to the right. The whole section was dark but I silently checked it anyway. Systematically, I moved around all of Domenica's front rooms. No one was waiting for me in the shadows.

Access to the kitchen was possible through two doors, one just off the dance floor, the other in the dining room. The swinging door between the kitchen and the dining room was identical to the door near the stage I had come through earlier when I was dragged from the car by Julian's punks. I inched the swinging door open, careful not to make any noise, and stepped into the kitchen. The only light in the kitchen came from a long hallway on the left reaching back into the rear of the building. Only half of the fluorescent lights in the hallway were lit. The appliances around me used the dim hall light to cast toothy shadows on the floor. I moved from one dark place to another, looking for any sign of the people who drove the two cars outside. Five metres down the hall that led to what must have been another back door was a single flimsy door, which spilled a brighter light out from underneath.

The door read MANAGER and inside two voices could be heard. I stood to the side of the door and listened. I could hear random words that were louder than others, like, "hospital" and "no," but nothing else was clear.

Before moving any farther, I pulled the digital recorder from my pocket. I turned the device on and slid it into my back pocket where the microphone could still pick up sound.

Once it was firmly in my pocket, I stopped wasting time. Mickey and Ralphy would be coming back as fast as their feet could carry them. I went through the door foot first to find Julian behind a desk with a foot up. An old man was wrapping the foot until the Glock in my hand spoke its loud, single-syllable language to him.

"Jesus," Julian shouted. He stretched to see the old man's body fall to the floor. The movement caused the chair to tip, and he had to wave his hands frantically to get the necessary momentum to stay off the floor.

"Put your hands on the desk, Julian."

He stared at me until he decided to do what I had said.

"Okay. Yeah. I'm doing it."

"You lied to me, Julian. You said you were out of everything, and here I find out you still have your fingers in the pie."

"I didn't lie to anybody. I'm here in fucking Siberia where Paolo left me. This middle-of-nowhere club."

"You might be in the middle of nowhere, but you were still working an angle with Luca Perino. You and him were behind what happened to Army and Nicky. Your boys used their van when they went to see Luca and Paolo's nephews at Ave Maria."

I moved closer to the half-bandaged purple foot on the desk. Julian saw me looking at the foot. "You admiring your handiwork? What you did. Crippling me twice. You fucking hit me with a car, and what does that bastard do? He lets you walk. He lets you go and retires me. You worked for him for what? Years? I put in decades, and what does that old man give me for my loyalty? This shithole!"

"You didn't retire," I reminded him.

"'Cause he said so. No, I didn't. I'm not some old horse you just put out to pasture when he goes lame. I'm better than some stupid animal. Everybody knew that — except for Paolo. People remembered me. They respected what I did. They knew what I earned, and it wasn't this. People knew what happened to me wasn't right. I didn't put my time in so some outsider could take me out. Paolo made some enemies that day."

"So why not go after him? Why Army and Nicky?"

Julian stared at his dead foot. "He made enemies, but they weren't going to go up against their boss. No one would stand for that. Paolo had to fall. He had to hang himself. Take himself out. Fall from grace. Then he could die."

Julian's words rattled in my brain, and all at once I saw his angle. "You knew what he would do if you killed Army and Nicky?"

Despite the pain in his foot, Julian nodded and laughed.

"You got Luca Perino to help you make a play on the boys knowing Paolo would go after his lieutenants under the table."

"After he retired me, he had no help left. No one he could trust."

"You didn't know he'd get me," I said.

"If it wasn't you, it would have been somebody else. That old man would go after his own people in a heart-beat. I mean, look how he treated me just for getting hurt. Imagine what he'd do to someone he thought deserved it. Someone who went after his nephews. His *family*." He spat when he said "family." "See how he treats family? The hypocrite. Everyone saw where Paolo's loyalties lay when he screwed me. They saw what happened to me. Everyone saw!"

"So you got in Luca Perino's ear," I said, imagining the events taking place in my mind.

"I showed him the writing on the wall. He knew what was coming. It was only a matter of time till he had a shitty club of his own."

"He didn't see all of it. You were going to use him to kill Paolo, weren't you?" Julian said nothing so I kept going. "You convinced him to kill Paolo's family with you, and when Paolo went crazy you would convince Perino the time was right to take out the boss too."

Julian stared at me hard, letting me know I was on track.

"I bet you still have contacts with the rest of the big players in other cities. You'd tell them that Paolo had gone off the deep end. He went after his own guys and started an internal war. Then you'd tell them that you could clean everything up and get things back to the way things should be. The other families would just want business as usual, and you figured they'd use you because you were a name they could trust. A name that earned more than it got. You were going to parlay that grip on a cane into a grip on the city."

Julian still said nothing. His hands stayed in his lap, and his destroyed foot stayed on the desk. I looked down at the man on the floor and then back to Julian. His eyes were on the Glock pointed at him. He wanted to get up and take it, but he knew his body wouldn't let him. He stared at the gun until he saw my left hand pull the tape recorder from my pocket. I clicked it off and held it in my hand.

"You took a big chance with all of this."

Julian looked at the recorder as he spoke. "I spent my life putting Paolo up. Me. My muscles, my sweat, my blood is what let that old man sit in his comfy restaurant and spout off about fucking animals all day. It was no chance that I took. It was an experiment, survival of the meanest. Heh, Paolo loves experiments, and this one was right up his alley. I wanted to see if that old man could keep order in his own house. If he could, then I belong where I am. But if he couldn't take care of his own, then his seat belongs to me because I put him there."

Julian's experiment went just like he thought it would. Paolo turned on his own people without a second thought. Just like he turned on Julian. Just like he would turn on me.

"You know Army and Nicky have family in Buffalo. Big shots."

"Yeah, I know. Pop Guillermo, their cousin, is over there. So what. How's he helping me. What's he done for me?"

"I'm saying this tape gets loose, Paolo won't matter. If he doesn't get you, someone else will."

"There's always someone," he said.

"Luca Perino is dead," I said as I put the recorder away in my pocket.

Julian looked up at me, confused; he didn't understand what I was saying. I didn't try to explain myself. Instead, I pulled out the phone and dialled the number I had called more than once over the past few days. Paolo answered on the second ring. After he spoke I said, "I know what happened. Everything."

"Where are you?"

"Place called Domenica's. You know it?"

"'Course I know it. I gave it to Julian. Why are you there?"

"I have everything wrapped up here. You need to come here and finish this. This can only end with you." I hung up the phone before he could reply.

Julian stared at me. His jaw worked back and forth, grinding his teeth down. I put the cell phone in my back pocket and pulled out the revolver I took off Johnny, the pointy-shoed messenger, endless days ago. I put the Glock under my armpit and wiped the revolver clean with my shirt. I put Johnny's gun, still loaded, on the corner of the big desk and waited for Julian to look away from it to me.

"This is your chance to have one less someone. But if you come after me in any way," I said, patting the recorder in my pocket, "this will make sure I don't come back for you alone."

I backed out the door, watching Julian watch the gun.

As I moved into the dining room, I could hear Julian grunting as he tried to get at the gun. After a minute of what must have been agony, the noise stopped — Julian had something more deadly than a working foot. I let Julian live because there was too much about him that I didn't know. How many more people like Luca Perino was he involved with? How many other people knew I was back in the city? If others like Julian knew I was involved with Paolo and the attacks on two of his lieutenants, I would never be safe. Worse, Steve and Sandra would never be out of danger. People would use them to get at me. People with less restraint than Paolo. Keeping Julian alive, but on a leash, was the best way to survive. Julian's sins against two made kids gave me what I needed to cage the hobbled beast. He would not come after me like Paolo did. What I had on Julian would also keep Steve safe. He would no longer be a bargaining chip. Julian was my way out.

I went through the archway to the stage and moved into the deepest shadow I could find. In the dark, I waited. Minutes slowly turned on the clock mounted on the wall above the doorway. After the minute hand had worked its way halfway around the clock face, Paolo walked in — alone.

"*Figlio?*" Paolo whispered as he walked into the dining room. He never looked my way; he was focused on the kitchen, and the bright light spilling out of the office door I left open at the end of the dim hall. I watched him disappear into the kitchen and then move out of sight. I left the shadows and walked to the door. A single shot rang out in Domenica's as I left.

Outside, I dialled the phone and got an answer on the second ring.

"Sully's Tavern."

"It's finished," I said.

"No, it's not. He's still out there in his car."

"He needs to disappear without a trace. No one can see him go. Can you do that?"

Steve didn't answer or hang up. The hard plastic phone just landed on the bar. Once again he was loose. I hoped it would be the last time.

I ended the call and walked away from Domenica's towards Ave Maria and the car I left behind. The car would still be there. It was too far away for anyone to notice it. There would not be cops around it, either, because the woman at Ave Maria knew what kind of men she worked for; she wouldn't call in any suspicious gunshots. As I walked, I took apart the phone and lost it piece by piece. The gun went next. All that was left was me, but I couldn't lose myself in the city so easily.